"I'm going to kiss you, Abby."

"Uh-huh."

He loved the way she didn't hesitate with her response, though her face flushed, and the pulse at the side of her neck started racing.

It was a hard, dry kiss. Not satisfying by a long shot, but he didn't want to presume any more than he already had. He could still remember the shock in her eyes fifteen years ago when his ex-wife made him sound like an animal. He didn't want to scare her away.

So, his heart skipped a beat when she whispered, "More. Please."

Nothing turned him on quite like a woman who knew what she wanted and wasn't afraid to ask for it. Except maybe this woman. Everything about her excited him. Grasping her shoulders and pulling her close, he slid his tongue along the seam of her lips until they opened, then delved into the warm recess of her mouth.

She met him with equal passion, and when her fingers slid beneath the brim of his hat, scraping the sides of his skull with her nails, a sizzle raced up his spine. He was a teenage boy again. On fire with lust for her like it was the first time he ever held a woman; he was ready to put the car seats back and fog up the windows.

This is a work of fiction. Names, characters, places, and incidents are either the product of the author's imagination or are used fictitiously, and any resemblance to actual persons living or dead, business establishments, events, or locales, is entirely coincidental.

Precedent for Passion (revised)
COPYRIGHT © 2024 by Amber Cross
Written by Amber Cross
All rights reserved. No part of this book may be used or reproduced in any manner whatsoever without written permission of the author, except in the case of brief quotations embodied in critical articles or reviews.
Cover Art by Ashlyn Chase at ashlynchase.com[1]
Previous Publishing History
The Wild Rose Press, 2018

---

1.   http://ashlynchase.com

Precedent for Passion
by
Amber Cross

Love in the Kingdom Series
Book One

Chapter One

Clutching her jacket closed with one hand at her neck and another at her knees, Abby Wilson shuffled backward toward the steepled white church at the end of the common. A gust of wing slapped her in the face and tore the breath from her lungs. Fairy lights danced from the nude maple trees lining the sidewalk, winking at her like they knew the punch line to a joke she hadn't yet heard.

Turning to see how far she had to go, she shuffled along faster.

Icy pellets falling from the gunmetal-gray sky stung her eyes. She blinked and pulled her lips in, taking shallow breaths through her nose.

So much for getting dolled up. She could almost feel her waterproof mascara running and her guaranteed not to smudge lipstick smudging.

She had spent a lot of time on her appearance this morning. This wedding provided a rare chance for her to wear something other than the black robe that hid her figure when she sat behind the bench or the nondescript pantsuits she favored when meeting clients at her law practice. She usually scraped her hair back into a tight bun and wore a minimum amount of makeup. Ugly plastic glasses she didn't need went one step further to camouflaging any hint of sexuality. At less than five feet tall, with an ample top and even curvier bottom, she needed people to take her seriously.

Not today.

The silky, teal-blue dress beneath her jacket would shock Judge Henry and her feminist mother. They would raise their eyebrows at the calf-enhancing heels on her feet. Sexy, impractical shoes that made her skid on the icy sidewalk.

Behind her the church bell tolled.

Oh, no.

She was already late, thanks to a last-minute phone call from Judge Henry, but she could hardly tell her mentor she didn't have time to talk.

He might think she was joining the throngs of people rushing to retail outlets for Black Friday sales, something he would view as shallow and nonjudicial. Telling him she was attending a wedding would be almost as bad, maybe worse. After decades spent presiding over family court, he had nothing but contempt for the state of matrimony in Vermont.

She didn't share his cynicism. She also didn't want to thank the bride and groom for their invitation by being the last guest seated.

Shivering, she hurried faster.

"Hold up! Hold up!" a man in a wool overcoat shouted when she stepped through the gate onto the church walkway.

The sudden stop caused her heels to skate across the uneven brick surface. To keep from falling, she reached for the picket fence and let go of her jacket. It was decorative outerwear with only a clasp at the collar, and the sides flapped like crow's wings into the air. Cold wind molded her dress to her knees, thighs, and breasts, and her nipples reacted to the frigid assault, hard points pushing against the thin fabric.

Her face flamed.

The man approaching her didn't seem to notice, his gaze falling to her generous curves. It seemed to be more of a reflexive action than a lascivious one, though, and when he jerked his head up his cheeks were ruddy.

Abby pulled one side of her jacket across her body.

"Sorry, ma'am," the young man met her gaze now. "Hear that bell?"

Of course, that's why she was hurrying.

"I think that means the bride is about to go down the aisle."

Abby looked closely at him. He was maybe, just maybe, old enough to buy alcohol; obviously too young to know a tolling bell was the last call for people to come to church before a ceremony begins.

"Let her in, Bryce," a deep voice near the door called out. With the wind and rain, she hadn't realized anyone else was outside.

Bryce nodded for her to go in. She clutched her coat together and picked her way across the bricks toward the entrance while the bell tolled above her.

"Bride or groom?"

Abby wasn't sure of her answer. Jason Hunter was her neighbor and fellow planning board member. She had served as a one-time real estate broker for Sara Tewskbury. The invitation to their wedding had come as a flattering surprise.

"Ma'am?"

Making sure her feet were solidly and safely planted on the icy walkway, she looked up at the man on the steps, suddenly understanding the phrase, *weak in the knees.*

A thatch of dark curls fell over his high forehead. A trim beard and mustache enhanced his strong jaw. In a form-fitting tuxedo with an aster poking out of the lapel to match his light blue gaze, he made her mouth water.

Glen Plankey.

For fifteen years his face had fueled her late-night fantasies. When the bed was too big, and the world too lonely, she imagined his body covering her own.

He recognized her. She could tell by the flicker of his eyes before he controlled the reaction. "Are you a guest of the bride or the groom?"

"Both, I suppose."

He opened the door and said to someone inside, "Put her in Sara's section."

He held the door open above her, his height allowing her to pass beneath him without any contact, and she followed an usher inside. She was proud of herself for not once looking over her shoulder.

The church bell stopped tolling.

Glen came up the aisle and joined two other men at the altar. She recognized them as Jason's son, Andrew and Sara's best friend, Jimmy. When Jason stepped up beside them, he lifted a violin to his shoulder, and a hush fell over the assembly as the first chords of Mendelssohn's wedding tune floated through the air.

The congregation rose to their feet.

Abby and the other guests watched two children precede the bride down the center aisle. They were clean and polished and their eyes darted about nervously. Unlike Sara. Her smile rivaled the church lighting when she saw her groom waiting for her.

A collective sigh passed through the guests. In a simple gown made of candle glow satin, carrying a wreath of white chrysanthemums and blue asters, she was radiant.

Abby harbored a secret love of weddings. As a teenager she'd hidden bride magazines from her activist mother and nontraditional father, who never wed and abhorred all things traditional. She hadn't mentioned it in law school for fear of classmates thinking she only wanted a degree to land a rich husband. In her working life there was no place for such conversations, but she never doubted her own day would come. Eventually it would be her turn to walk down the aisle and exchange vows with the man of her dreams.

She turned her head to the front of the church. All three of the male attendants were tall and good looking, but her gaze went right to Glen Plankey. In his black tuxedo with the satin lapel, he could have been a model for any of the glossy magazines she'd tucked beneath her mattress all those years ago.

Had he remarried after that bitter divorce? Part of her hoped so. She wanted him to be happy, because any man who suffered the kind of humiliation he had been through deserved happiness, but another part of her hoped he was single. Although she would probably never have a conversation with him, she could fantasize about him without feeling guilty if he was single; something she did throughout the wedding ceremony.

She had never thought of a man's back as particularly sexy; his was. Long and lean, it narrowed to a trim waist just before his tailored jacket flared to cover his backside, and what a backside! She could tell it was toned even before he reached into his pants pocket to retrieve the ring for Jason. What that movement did for his body and her imagination could be a crime. Maybe it was, but not in her jurisdiction.

"I give you Mr. and Mrs. Jason Hunter!"

Snapped out of her preoccupation by the minister's announcement, Abby lifted her head only to have her gaze snared by a pair of blue eyes. Her face heated with embarrassment. Nothing like being caught in the act, and in church no less.

Maybe he wasn't single after all.

He broke eye contact, thumped Jason on the back then kissed Sara on the cheek. She was several inches taller than Abby yet managed to look diminutive between his six and a half feet and Jason's equally tall son. When the younger man bent her over his arm and gave her a thorough kiss, the Man of Honor let out a loud hooligan's call echoed by several guests in the pews.

Abby was shocked, yet Jason had an indulgent smile on his face. Sara laughed, swatted her stepson's arm, and was immediately returned to her husband.

"Boy's got good taste," Glen Plankey exclaimed.

The whole congregation laughed.

A pang of disappointment went through Abby. If his taste ran to women like Sara, his marital status was irrelevant because she would never measure up. She wasn't lean and athletic. She didn't have an easy, laid-back way about her. Her job was her life, and her only real talent was her intelligence, not exactly a turn-on for most men.

"They're going to take photographs now," the woman beside Abby said.

"What?"

"We have to leave now." Waving her hands, she indicated Abby should vacate the pew ahead of her. "The wedding party is being photographed. We need to go to the reception hall."

"Oh."

Disappointed, because she wouldn't get to see more of the best man, and relieved, because she wouldn't see him and be tempted by her own wayward thoughts, Abby exited the pew and then the church.

****

Glen Plankey couldn't believe his luck. The one woman on the planet capable of ruining his day more than his ex-wife was here at his best friend's wedding. How did she know Jason and Sara? She wasn't close to them, he could tell by her answer to the seating question. Was she crashing the party? He lived in New York City and saw all sorts of cons and swindles, but they could happen in the Northeast Kingdom just as easily. After all, his ex had pulled off one of the biggest scams in Essex County, and this woman had a front row seat to it.

She had changed in the fifteen years since then. It didn't matter. He would know those gray-green eyes anywhere. He could still remember the shock in them when he was verbally castrated before the judge, his pride shattered, his dreams torn to shreds. Even now he wanted to wrap his fist in her thick chestnut hair and force her to look up and see him for the man he was instead of the monster his ex-wife made him out to be. He hated her for being witness to that. He hated her reaction. Most of all, he hated himself for noticing or caring what she thought.

Glen watched her leave with the other guests and sighed with relief. Now he could give all his attention to Jason and Sara, where before he had one eye on the wedding ceremony and one on the voluptuous little brunette in the tenth row. He knew exactly which row she was in. Pathetic, especially considering the way she looked at him when Andrew kissed Sara. What right did she have to look down on their lighthearted fun, to pass judgment on them? He wanted to shake her and stamp the shock from her face.

Instead, he forced himself to engage in what was going on around him.

He was here to celebrate his best friend's nuptials and strangling one of the guests was out of the question.

Despite his own miserable and miserably short marriage, he still believed in the institution. He just didn't believe in it for himself.

"Smile for the camera," Jason said.

Twenty minutes later Glen and the rest of the wedding party dispersed into the bitter cold to find their cars behind the church covered with a thin layer of ice. While drivers started engines, he and Jason scraped their windshields.

The exertion felt good. Every time he shoved the blade of the scraper across the glass, some of the anger blossoming inside him lessened.

He shouldn't let the woman get to him, yet his emotions were out of control and had been since seeing her gray-green eyes at the church doors. Maybe even before that when her lush body was exposed to the cold by the wind. He thought his poor nephew Bryce was going to have a stroke on seeing that, which was why he came to the boy's rescue and told him to let her in. His reaction was just as bad.

Normally he dated women who were chic, and lean, and within a few inches of his height. Since when did generous curves on an otherwise petite form hold such fascination for him? He didn't understand any more than he understood why a fifteen-year memory should still provoke such a visceral response from him.

"This is good luck, right?" Jason asked.

"How's that?" They were side by side, Jason scraping the windshield of his jeep while Glen cleared his own BMW.

"Bad weather on a wedding day is supposed to mean a long and happy marriage."

"I don't think you have anything to worry about." The twelve-year age difference between them him and Sara didn't matter. They were two halves of one whole. "You deserve her, man. I don't think you need any luck."

"Why, thank you," Sara said, approaching from the back door of the church. She had changed out of her wedding gown and carried a gym bag in her hand. Tossing it into the jeep, she came around to where he was scraping the back window. "Glen?"

"Hmm?"

"Thank you." She stretched up on her tiptoes and kissed his cheek.

"What's that for?"

"For being such a good friend to both of us."

A sudden lump in his throat kept him from speaking. He and Jason had been inseparable from first grade. When his whole life fell apart, Jason stood by him without any doubt, questions, or recriminations. Glen would like anyone who made his friend happy, but his affection for Sara was as much about who she was.

"You've left him speechless," Jason teased, opening the passenger door for her to get in. Before closing it, he gave her a kiss, adding, "Nicely done."

Glen found his tongue again. "Does this mean I don't have to stand up in front of everyone at the hall and say ridiculously flattering things about you?"

"You can't get out of best man speech that easily."

"Okay, okay." Opening his car door, he tossed the scraper behind the driver's seat. "I'll try to come up with something."

"Remember that we don't have a wedding party table. Sara wanted people to mix and mingle, so she arranged seats based on who she thought would enjoy talking to each other."

Glen understood her intentions, but when he arrived at the hall, he wished she had been more traditional because the card with his name on it was right across from a mane of chestnut hair and form-flattering, teal-blue dress.

****

Abby couldn't believe her good fortune when the usher directed her to a table at the reception and she read the name opposite her own. That is, until she read the one beside it. *Linda Plankey*. Not single then; not just temporarily off the market, either, but married. Well, what had she expected? If a straight man like him was unattached, her gender had a lot to answer for.

"Can I take your coat for you?" the usher asked. It was the same young man she'd met outside the church, and he was unusually tall. As short as she was, even if she stood up to remove her coat, he would have an unobstructed view of her cleavage in the surplice wrap dress.

"Why don't you just show me where to put it?" That way she wouldn't make either one of them uncomfortable again. Aloud, she said, "Then I can use the rest room at the same time."

A few minutes later she returned to her seat, hair detangled and smoothed down, makeup repaired. Six empty champagne flutes had been delivered to the table, but so far no one else had joined her, which meant she had to sit still with nothing to do. She considered taking a pen out of her purse and scribbling on the paper napkin or checking her cell phone for news that wasn't important.

"Don't do it," she muttered even as her finger played with the zipper on her bag. It would be rude. She knew it would, but boredom made her crazy. She rarely did one thing and one thing only. Whether it was talking on the phone with a client or watching a movie at home, she also did a crossword puzzle, a Sudoku, even knitting—she knew how to knit and purl but not finish anything, so it was simply knitting—to keep both her brain and her hands occupied.

"Hello there," a man with steely hair and kind brown took the chair next to hers. "You must be"—he paused to read her card— "Abby."

"I am." She was relieved to have company.

"Then I guess that makes me Neil Swain." He extended a hand and she shook it. "Nice to meet you, Abby."

"You, too."

Being an attorney and judge, she was good at asking questions that gave other people an opening to talk at length about themselves. In no time she learned Neil was a highway crew manager and his wife was Jason's secretary at the quarry. "Greta's helping out in the kitchen," he said, referring to her now. "I imagine Linda is too, but Glen and Jimmy should be here as soon as the wedding pictures are done."

She might have said something, or not, because just then six and a half feet of dark-haired, blue-eyed distraction arrived, pulling out the chair across the table from her and turning her normally sharp brain to mush.

He greeted Neil by name, glanced over the place card with her name yet made no eye contact. Maybe he was embarrassed? After all, she had been checking out his rear end during the ceremony.

Neil pushed his chair back and stood. "Now you're here to keep Abby company, I'm going to see if Greta needs a hand."

His departure left behind an awkward silence. Glen Plankey's gaze fixed on a spot over her shoulder while her fingers pulled idly at the zipper on her bag. When she realized what she was doing, she decided one of them had to break the ice, and it might as well be her. "Will your wife be joining us soon?"

Blue eyes snapped to her face, and she almost recoiled from the anger in them. "Is that your idea of a joke?"

Whoa! She had his attention now. Before she could figure out why such a simple question caused such a visceral reaction, the two remaining guests from his side of the table arrived.

Jimmy Duncan took the woman's coat and wool cap, disappearing with them while she slid into the seat beside Glen. Abby surreptitiously observed her. She was tall, with a lean, muscular body and ruddy features that spoke to hours spent outside without moisturizer. Her dark hair, when she shook it free of hat marks, was thick and curled loosely to just below her chin. Something about her was also familiar, like maybe they had met before but in another setting.

Nothing about her behavior indicated a significant relationship with Glen. Abby detected no hint of a romantic attachment. In fact, they hadn't even spoken to one another yet. Was he going through another divorce? That would explain the hostile response to her innocent question.

Jimmy Duncan returned, smiling affably across the table at her. "Hey, Judge."

"You're a *judge*?"

What now? Abby was used to surprise from people when they found out what she did for work, but nothing like this. Most of the time it was due to her age, because she was only thirty-five and had been on the bench for almost two years. Sometimes it was because she was a woman. If she had to describe Glen's reaction, she would say it was somewhere between shock and revulsion.

The woman stuck her hand across the table. A deliberate interruption. "Hi. I'm Linda Plankey."

Abby shook her hand automatically. She would have introduced herself as well, but two young people rushed up to the table with the usher. He was the first to speak. "Uncle Glen, is it okay if we go to Jason's place for a minute? We'll be right back."

"What for?"

"He forgot the wine!" the teenage girl wailed, her pretty face reflecting disbelief that anyone could be so careless on a wedding day.

All eyes turned to Jimmy. "Uh-oh."

"Please, Dad?" the girl pressed, blue eyes imploring. "Jason said it's right inside the door and you'll need it for the toasts."

"We'll be quick," the usher promised.

"That's what I'm afraid of. It's icy out there."

The third young person pushed his way between the other two. Tall with wide, bony shoulders holding up a New York Rangers jersey and a narrow jaw still unblemished by facial hair, he said with a slash of white teeth, "If it will make you feel any better, I'll drive."

Glen shuddered dramatically. "Nice try, son." To his nephew he said, "You can drive but be careful. The town crew was treating the roads when we got here, but they're still slippery."

They left in a flurry of energy, one last caution following them to the door.

"Just to Jason's and back."

Abby needed a cardiologist. Or a shrink. Or both. Because when he lowered his voice to issue the stern warning, everything inside her clenched. She bit her lower lip and took a deep breath. It was either that or give voice to the moan welling up inside her because if one thing turned her on, it was an authoritative man.

What was *wrong* with her? She shouldn't find anything about him attractive. He had acted like a jerk moments before, but when he smiled after the young people, her heart flip-flopped.

He's married. Keep it up, and you'll have a jealous wife to contend with.

A quick glance showed Linda Plankey eyeing her with speculation. Great. First, she was caught looking at his backside, now she was caught salivating over him. Someone needed to save her from herself, and that someone took the form of Neil Swain returning with a gray-haired lady who could only be his wife. Even better, his first words were "Glen, Jason needs you backstage."

Abby was glad to see him go. Her emotions had been bouncing all over the place, and his absence would let her get them under control.

Unfortunately, Linda Plankey had other ideas. "Don't take his reaction to your job personally. He's not fond of judges, but that's not why he acted that way."

Abby didn't want to discuss him with his wife, but the woman wasn't done.

"He has to give a speech," she said as if that explained everything.

Desperate to change the subject, Abby said, "I'm sure your husband is a nice guy—"

"Husband?"

From the stage a microphone squealed, capturing everyone's attention. Jason Hunter tapped on the electronic device before speaking. "Ladies and gentlemen, can I have your attention please?"

The room went quiet. Glen Plankey walked onto the stage with a second microphone and a guitar in his hand.

"It seems someone forgot the wine for the toasts." Jason peered directly at Jimmy, and the guests laughed. "Since the best man can't give a speech until it gets here, we're going to change the order of the program. Sara, will you join me up here? I have a surprise for you." When she looked reluctant to leave her seat, he added, "Come on. I dare you."

"Smart man." Jimmy laughed. "She can't resist a challenge."

Once Sara settled on the piano bench, Glen tuned his guitar, and Jason stepped closer to his microphone. "Now I have a special gift for my bride."

Abby understood the song choice immediately. Like her, Jason was in his thirties and had never married. Unlike her, he was a single father. He had all but given up hope of sharing his life with anyone other than Andrew when he finally found "the one."

Jason's baritone voice filled the hall, mesmerizing the guests, but she couldn't stop looking at the guitarist. Dark curls fell across his forehead as he bent to the instrument. His long fingers plucked and stroked the strings, and she wondered how they would play a woman's body.

The lyrics spoke to finally being close to *the one*; the only one.

She could appreciate that sentiment. After fifteen years of fantasizing about Glen Plankey, seeing him in the flesh again made those dreams pale by comparison. She would take him smiling, rude, authoritative; she would take him any way at all, if he would only give her half the attention he was giving to the guitar in his hands.

If only he wasn't married.

A collective sigh went through the room as Jason finished the lyrics with a promise to make Sara's happiness his life's mission.

Abby exhaled a breath she didn't know she was holding and blinked herself back to the present. She stood with the other guests and cheered for the bride and groom. When Glen's nephew hopped up onto the stage holding a bottle of wine in each hand, they cheered again before chanting, "Speech, speech, speech."

Within minutes every table had champagne glasses filled, and Glen Plankey was alone at the microphone. He cleared his throat. The room went quiet. He ran his hand through his hair, pushed it off his forehead, and cleared his throat a second time.

He's nervous.

As if she had made the observation aloud, Linda explained, "He hates speaking in front of a crowd."

Suddenly Abby remembered him standing before Judge Henry at the courthouse in Guildhall. Much younger, as handsome then as now and just as nervous, he had tripped over his words while trying to defend himself against his wife's accusations. Explaining that what happened in their bedroom, as kinky as it sounded to her virginal ears, had nothing to do with his parenting skills and should not affect custody of their children.

Chapter Two

The lump in Glen's throat seemed to paralyze his vocal cords. He tried clearing it twice. If he did it a third time, he'd look as foolish as he felt.

The wedding guests merged into a formless void. The microphone in his hands was damp from perspiration, but he couldn't let go because he was shaking so much. Each breath roared loud in his ears.

In full-fledged panic attack, he looked for an escape, any escape, his gaze finally lighting on the piano bench where Jason and Sara sat waiting.

Cupping her hand to her cheek so no one else could see, she mouthed one word. "Harness."

Processing the word was like wading through his brother's manure bin after a heavy rain. He had to repeat it in his head several times before remembering what it meant.

Sara was a speech language pathologist. Knowing how he dreaded making this speech, she had coached him to harness his emotions, good or bad, and use them to power through his anxiety.

Taking a deep breath, he nodded and returned his attention to the room full of people.

He could do this. For her. For Jason.

Bodies took shape. Faces came into focus. One face in particular captured his attention, fueling the angst and anger inside him. How he wanted to hate that beautiful face. Remembering her lush mouth falling open, her cheeks turning pink, and her gray-green eyes going wide while she listened to his ex-wife fifteen years ago, he imagined instead another scenario. One where those lips were on his body, those eyes drowning with pleasure, those cheeks pink for an entirely different reason.

Buoyed by the images, he began. "When I was a boy, I stuttered. The doctor said it was because I was a genius and was thinking faster than I could talk, but the school didn't agree and kept me back a year.

My teacher decided that a learning partner might help, and she paired me up with the smartest kid in class for my second round of first grade."

Abby's elbows rested on the table. Because she was short, her breasts pressed against the edge and spilled over into the V of her dress, adding to his fantasy and giving him strength to continue.

"It was the best thing anyone ever did for me. I got to sit with Jason Hunter through the rest of elementary school. And though I might be a genius, he's still the smartest man I know. Like a wise old owl."

The crowd murmured their agreement.

"Only a wise man would save himself for marriage like he did. And only a smart man would recognize his soul mate the first time he met her."

Smiling at Sara's obvious surprise, he went on. "That's right. The very first night, after seeing you at The Gables, he called me and told me you were the one. He was afraid he might never run into you again. You see, he doesn't have my talent for flirting with pretty women, so of course he needed my expert advice." Glen winked, she blushed, and the wedding guests laughed.

"Seriously, though, he was afraid he wouldn't have a chance with you, him being so *old* and all. I told him any woman, even a young one, would be a fool to turn him down. Then I met you the next summer when I came up for haying on the Fourth of July. You two were going through a rough patch then, but the chemistry between you was hotter than the fireworks that night."

The crowd laughed when he waggled his eyebrows suggestively.

"I knew you belonged together. In all the years we've been friends, I've never seen Jason so happy. You've done that for him. And at the risk of swelling his head, he's about as good as a guy can get. He deserves you."

Jason nodded to him, a silent thank you for the heartfelt compliment.

"Please stand and join me," Glen said to the guests, waiting until they rose, and Jimmy gave him a glass of champagne. "Here's to Jason and Sara. A perfect match. May they have many happy years together!"

They drank to his toast. Jason stood and thumped him on the back. Sara kissed him on the cheek and hugged him tight, which was good because the relief of being done made him weak. When Jimmy took the mic and he stepped down from the stage, his legs were shaking.

Back at the table he drained his champagne flute in one swallow without even sitting down.

"More?" Linda asked.

Her dry tone penetrated the freefall he was in after the adrenaline rush from being on stage.

"Sorry." He kissed the top of her head. Abby jerked like someone slapped her.

Linda handed him the bottle of wine. Absently he took it and seated himself, but his gaze was on the woman with the chestnut hair and teal dress. She seemed to be fiercely concentrating on Jimmy's speech, ignoring him the way he had tried earlier to ignore her.

"It's called Good in Bed," Linda said.

"What?" She had his attention now.

"The wine. Jason had some on a trip to Washington State, so they ordered it through a New York seller for the wedding because we can't get it here in Vermont. It's called Good in Bed."

Why was she telling him this? She didn't usually make random conversation, even to help him through a public speaking event.

"Abby thinks we're married."

The wine and Jimmy's speech were forgotten as both he and the little judge whipped their heads up to look at one another. She looked startled. A flush stained her cheeks.

"Glen's my big brother."

Oh.

The question about his wife joining him made sense now. She wasn't being rude.

Say something.

He could almost hear the encouraging words coming from his sister. Normally he was good with females. He hadn't been joking about that in his speech, but now he found himself tongue-tied. A combination of high emotion from being on stage and fifteen years of resenting this woman only to use fantasies about her to help him through that ordeal. So, what came out of his mouth was simply the first thing he could think of.

"Your hair is curling." When she gave him a blank look, he explained, "At the side of your face, by your ears."

Her blush deepened, and she twirled one of the ringlets around a finger, stretching it out straight then letting it pop back into place. "It happens when I'm in a room full of people and it's warm, or when it's humid outside."

He admired the way the curls clung to her cheeks and the smooth golden skin of her neck.

"It's the black in me coming out."

****

"Can you check on Abby for me?"

Glen had just settled into Jason's vacated condo unit. The last thing he wanted was to cross the hall and check on the judge. Even big, gray-green eyes and a luscious, little body couldn't compensate for an ugly soul.

He never wanted to see her again after that racist comment at the wedding reception two weeks ago.

"There's a creeper in town," Jason explained, "stalking women who live alone. The police have asked us to check on anyone in that category, and I said I'd check on Abby, but her phone is going right to voicemail. Can you knock on her door and make sure she's okay?"

"You do know what time it is, right?" Long past midnight. "She could be sleeping."

"Not on a Friday night. It takes her hours to unwind after the workweek."

"And you know this because?"

"Don't even go there. We were neighbors for almost two years, nothing else, but I'd like to make sure my former neighbor isn't under attack from some crazy predator. Now, are you going to do this, or do I have to leave my wife alone and at risk to check on her myself?"

Exhaling a rough breath to make sure Jason knew it was inconvenient, he gave in. "I'll do it." As if there were any other reply he could make.

Tossing the phone onto the sofa sleeper that would be his bed until he could get some more furniture delivered, he slid his feet into soft leather moccasins and reluctantly covered his naked torso with a faded T-shirt. With flannel pajama pants, it wasn't his usual New York GQ style, but he wasn't out to impress anyone.

Across the square hall, he lifted the old-fashioned brass pull on the door to her unit and listened while "Carol of the Bells" chimed from inside.

Minutes passed. The doorbell was the last and only sound he heard from inside the apartment. Was she asleep? Maybe she was getting dressed in a back room.

He paced the eight-by-eight-feet of hardwood flooring and tried the doorbell again when enough time had passed that she could have put on clothes and makeup too.

Still no answer. They were on the third floor. No one could get up here without a security code, so what was Jason worried about, anyway? For all he knew the woman might be out of town. Deciding he had done his duty, Glen was about to return to his apartment when the elevator door pinged open.

"Put your hands up!"

"What the—?" Shocked, he stared uncomprehendingly as a stocky policewoman advanced out of the elevator car with one hand on the butt of a service weapon at her hip. "I repeat. Put. Your. Hands. Up. And step away from the door."

Dumbfounded, Glen did as he was told.

"Now turn and put your hands against the wall."

Still stunned, he automatically tried to reason with her. "Officer, I think there's been a mistake."

"Against the wall!"

Wondering if he was being pranked, he nonetheless turned and placed his hands as directed.

The woman frisked him! Ran her hands down his sides, over his torso, and up the inside of his thighs. What did she think he was hiding in these clothes? "You're making a mistake," he told her.

She ignored that as if he hadn't spoken. "What are you doing in this apartment building?"

"I live here."

"Wrong answer, pal. There are only two condos up here, and I know both owners. You're not one of them."

He turned to explain, but she yelled at him not to move so he spoke to the wall instead. With exaggerated patience, as if he were addressing a small child. "My name is Glen Plankey. Jason sublet his unit to me when he got married. I live in New York and came up for the weekend." His first time since the wedding, and it wasn't working out too well so far.

"Why were you breaking into Judge Wilson's condo?"

"Breaking in?" Glen was getting irritated now, and it showed in his reply. "Since when is ringing the doorbell a crime?"

"I'm asking the questions. Why were you ringing the doorbell?"

Taking a deep breath, reaching for a calm he didn't feel, he said, "Jason called and asked me to. He said there's been a sexual predator around town, and everyone is checking on women who live alone to make sure they're okay. When the judge didn't answer her phone, he asked me to make sure she's all right."

"That should be easy enough to verify."

He started to lower his hands, but to his surprise a cuff circled his wrist followed by a click, then she yanked both of his arms behind his back. Every instinct told him to resist, but what good would that do? Another click and his wrists were secured. She turned him around with a hand at his elbow. "Sit."

The only thing on the floor was a leafy green plant in the corner by the window. It had been a six-hour drive up from the city, he was tired, and the last thing he wanted was to enter into a guessing game with this police officer. "Where would you suggest?"

Apparently, she didn't get sarcasm because she pursed her lips, looked around, and indicated the windowsill. "There."

Waiting until he backed up to the ledge and rested his hips on it, she pulled a cell phone from her breast pocket and punched in a number. She kept him in her sights while bringing the phone to her ear.

An answering ring came from inside the judge's condo unit. "This is B." Looking at him. "Officer Price." *To you* was indicated by her raised eyebrows and sour expression. "Can you step out here?"

A deadbolt slid free. The doorknob turned. Then *she* was there.

Annoyed and exhausted, Glen still reacted to the sight of her barefoot and dressed in a long nightshirt. Soft and kind to her curves, the pink fleece would be shapeless on anyone else. On her it made his mouth water. Only annoying him further, bringing him to his feet so he could tower over her and the other woman. His wrists were still cuffed, but it helped him reclaim some of his power.

Abby took one look at him and paled.

Good.

When her eyes dropped to his slippers and pajama pants, he could almost see her reaching the correct conclusion, that a man dressed like he was couldn't scale a three-story building.

"Hi, Judge." The officer's greeting got their attention. "This man says he sublet the other unit from Jason."

Abby's eyes widened, and she lost so much color he saw freckles on the bridge of her nose.

"Do you have Jason's number? I'll need him to confirm this."

She pulled a cell phone from her pocket, hands shaking as she punched in a series of numbers.

Glen heard two rings followed by a click, then Jason's voice filled the space between them.

"Hi Abby."

"Hey Jason." She hit the speakerphone button. "I've got B here with me." Throwing a nervous glance in his direction, she added, "Glen Plankey is here, too."

"Oh, good. I was worried when you didn't pick up your phone, so I asked him to make sure you were all right."

She glanced at his cuffed wrists but avoided eye contact.

"So, he is renting your condo?" Officer Price asked.

"Yeah. He didn't tell you that?"

"Of course, I told them." Closing the short gap between the window and Abby's doorway, he spoke directly to his friend, but kept his gaze fixed on the woman in pink. "For some reason this cop didn't believe me. I've got handcuffs on my wrists, and if my pretty skin has even one mark on it tomorrow, your face is going to have some too."

Jason's laughter filled the hall. "Nothing like a little kink on a Friday night, eh?"

Abby jerked, then stilled. She was probably remembering his ex-wife's lies from the courtroom.

"Just fix this mess so I can go back to minding my own business," Glen snapped.

"Okay. Can you put this poor man out of his misery, B? I'll vouch for him any time."

"Sure thing. Thanks for clearing this up. And for checking on our favorite judge."

"Yes," Abby said, "I appreciate it."

Glen wasn't about to say thank you. Let his best friend be the hero of the piece. He just wanted to get away from the overzealous policewoman and the tempting morsel in pink.

They disconnected the call.

With no apology for detaining him, Officer Price pulled a set of keys from her wide belt and indicated he should turn around so she could release the handcuffs. Glen didn't move. Let her circle him. He wasn't about to turn his back on these two and make himself any more vulnerable than he already was.

Whether or not he would have won that power play would remain a mystery because just then the policewoman's phone rang, and the call must have been important. She removed a key from the ring, dropped it into his palm, and moved to the corner by the window.

As if he could unlock the cuffs himself. It would be hard enough with traditional restraints, but these were the new ones, without a chain, and little give between his wrists. He couldn't even roll his hands in opposite directions, though he tried several times. With each failed attempt, his frustration mounted.

He needed an outlet.

He found one.

Walking right up to Abby, he forced her through the open door into her unit.

Gray-green eyes went wide. An intoxicating mix of musk and floral scents filled his lungs. He advanced until her back hit the wall and a mere sliver of space separated their bodies.

She swallowed. Was that fear he saw? Or were her pupils dilating for another reason?

If she was scared, she would call the policewoman. When she remained silent, he closed the gap between them.

A flush colored her cheeks and her eyelids flickered. She didn't look frightened at all. Instead, she looked...aroused.

He was experiencing a healthy dose of that himself. In her pink fleece, face free of makeup, she looked as soft and cuddly as any child's toy, but his interest in her was far from innocent. If she knew where his thoughts were wandering, she'd probably slap his face.

"Release me."

She inhaled sharply, her breasts expanding until they pressed into his chest. It was all he could do not to rub against them.

He was being a jerk, but he wanted to make her uncomfortable, to get his own back for her witnessing his downfall fifteen years ago, for the handcuffs, the suspicion, and for the inconvenience of being here when he should be sleeping across the hall.

"Take the key from my hand and release me."

He watched her swallow, fascinated by the smooth golden skin of her throat. Was it that color all over? It seemed too uniform to be natural. Maybe she used a tanning booth.

If she were a better person, he could really be enjoying this; a beautiful woman, a pair of handcuffs. It would make for great foreplay. But he was beyond the age where a woman's character was irrelevant as long as she was willing and eager. He didn't sleep with bimbos, and he certainly didn't sleep with racists.

"You'll have to turn around."

That breathless voice stroked across his senses and challenged his detachment. Affected despite his resolve, he all but growled, "I don't think so."

"What?"

"You heard me."

Her eyes went even wider, if possible, and she swallowed again. He didn't budge. She stood on her toes and tried looking around him, probably for the police officer, but his height made it impossible for her to see over his shoulder. Even if she could stretch that far, the other woman was still out in the hall. He could hear her talking on the phone.

"The sooner you release me, the sooner I'll be out of your way."

Her eyes met his gaze, then darted away. The color in her cheeks deepened. She tried reaching the cuffs by leaning slightly to one side. When that didn't work, she stretched one arm around him and managed to find the key in his palm, but as soon as she tried inserting it into the lock, the cuffs slid out of her grasp, and she ended up jabbing his lower back. Huffing in frustration, she finally wrapped both arms around his middle.

Sweet heaven. Glen closed his eyes and leaned his forehead against the wall above her as sensations overwhelmed him. How soft her body was in contrast to his, which was growing harder by the minute. To reach his hands she had to press her face against into the indentation at the top of his rib cage, and it was a perfect fit. Made for someone her size.

The cuffs fell away from his wrists. After shaking his hands and flexing his fingers, he placed both palms flat against the wall on either side of her head and drew back so he could see her.

She held the cuffs in one palm, the key in the other. When he didn't take them, a pulse beat wildly at the side of her throat.

"Do you want me to move away?" he taunted.

She glared at him, but he was shoving back from her, a violent action matching the disgust he felt. With himself, because until his breath stirred the ringlets by her ear, he had almost forgotten why he disliked her.

"Not much fun being trapped by someone else, is it? Boxed in? Cuffs, preconceived notions, expectations; they're all the same. All a trap."

****

What *was* his problem?

Abby was about to demand an explanation when Officer Price returned to her doorway. "Sorry about that," she said, "I had to take that call."

Collecting herself with effort, Abby managed what she hoped looked like a genuine smile. "That's okay. And thanks for coming, B. I appreciate it." Not looking at the man still too close for comfort, she returned the handcuffs and key to the policewoman. "I am sorry about this mess up. I took some Benadryl for a cold and was out like a light. I must not have heard the phone when Jason called."

"No problem." Poking her head around the doorway and looking into the living room, she said, "Nice place you got here."

"I like it." Right now she wanted to retreat inside and lock the door behind her, but that would be rude, especially after calling the woman out on a false alarm.

B motioned to a large portrait hanging from the far wall. "Who is the old black lady?"

Abby didn't want to answer. Not in front of him. The less he knew about her the better, but if she didn't reply she would have to explain her unusual behavior to B so reluctantly she said, "My grandmother."

"Your *grandmother*?"

The astonishment in his voice raised the hackles on the back of her neck. "Yes, my grandmother." Her defensive tone dared him to say something nasty about the woman she loved above all others.

Blue eyes narrowed. "How are you related?"

From astonishment to suspicion. *Jerk.* "She's my father's mother," she gritted out between clenched teeth.

"I thought you were a bigot."

"What?"

"You said your hair frizzes up when it's warm, and the black in you comes out. I thought you were making a bad joke; a racist one."

Abby digested that slowly, like she was trying a new food that started out bitter then improved, but she wasn't sure if she liked it enough to swallow.

He wasn't prejudiced.

"Am I missing something here?" B asked.

"Sorry." Abby realized they were having a private conversation in front of an audience.

B looked between them and nodded. "Okay, well, if you don't need me, I'll be off. Got paperwork, you know." Walking to the elevator while talking, she said, "You take care of that cold, Abby. There's a bad virus going around at the elementary school." She pushed the call button. "Half the kids in my little boy's class have been out with it." The car doors opened, and she stepped inside. "Watch out for this creep too, and don't hesitate to call if anything seems suspicious." She looked directly at Glen now. "Or anyone."

A wink softened her brusque manner, probably meant to take the sting out of her comment. "You two should exchange numbers. That way if you think someone's breaking in, you can call him, and if he needs to check on you, he doesn't have to knock on the door after midnight."

The elevator doors closed. An awkward silence followed her departure, broken only by the swish of the car descending to the first floor.

"I thought you were a racist," she finally admitted.

"Me?" He was clearly affronted. "Why would you think that?"

"You gave me such a dirty look when I said that about my hair curling, at the wedding. I thought you were prejudiced against black people."

"Oh." He seemed to think about their conversation for a minute. "I can understand that."

"The way you reacted, leaving the table and everything."

"Yeah." He nodded. "I just couldn't see any color in you."

Both fell silent. She knew her mixed race wasn't evident to most people.

He took a step back, out of her unit and into the hall. She could slam the door now and lock it behind her. Only she didn't want to. Despite everything that had happened, maybe because of it, she wanted to know who the real Glen Plankey was.

"Well"—he gestured with a hand toward his unit—"I guess I'll—"

"Can I buy you lunch?"

"Excuse me?"

She spoke at the same time he did, so maybe he hadn't heard her invitation. "Lunch," she repeated, "to make up for putting you out tonight. Can I buy you lunch tomorrow?"

He looked surprised, then uncomfortable, like he was searching for a polite way to say no.

"You're busy," she guessed.

"I'm working with my brother Roger at the farm." She hoped that was reluctance in his voice. "He's a dairyman. I came up to help him and Dad take care of some maintenance before winter sets in."

"Oh." She couldn't think of anything else to say, any other way to keep him.

"I'm free on Sunday."

She didn't even try to hide her happy reaction to that announcement. "That works for me. How about eleven o'clock at the Golden Dragon on Depot Street?"

His answering smile made her bare toes curl against the hardwood floor. "I'll be there."

Chapter Three

Red dress? Blue dress? Short dress? Long dress?

Like a Doctor Seuss riddle, the choices ran through Abby's brain as she emptied half the contents of her closet onto her bed on Saturday night. Dresses looked better on her short form than pants because they created long unbroken lines. Add a V neck and tights that matched the skirt in color, and she could visually fool people into thinking she was almost approaching an adult height. But she only owned two winter dresses; the teal one he had already seen, and a shapeless knit frock meant for doing errands on the weekend. A skirt and top would cut her in half and widen what looked better narrow, shorten what needed elongating.

Half an hour later she realized she was making herself nuts over what might not amount to anything more than a cordial lunch to bury the hatchet between them. So, she rolled a die, kept in her nightstand drawer just for big decisions like this, and when it landed on four, she pulled the fourth outfit from the mound of clothing on her comforter. A pair of wool tweed slacks and an Irish knit sweater. Ivory, with a turtleneck and intricate cabling down the front and along the arms, it wouldn't camouflage her diminutive stature or her round parts, but neither would it accentuate them.

Now she could finally go to bed and call it a night.

Or so she thought.

On Friday night she stayed up reliving her encounter with Glen, being close enough to feel his skin and breathe in his scent. Tonight wasn't looking any better.

Not only was he in the same building at this moment, but he would be there frequently. They could run into one another in the hall. Or the elevator.

If she left the door open to their shared balcony, would he accept the invitation and come over for a visit?

Of course, she wouldn't do that now. It was the middle of December and had been snowing since late afternoon.

That storm didn't stop until morning. She woke to several inches of heavy, wet snow on the balcony and nearby rooftops. According to the television newscast, it had brought tree limbs down on power lines and left the northeast part of town without electricity.

Her daily post-breakfast swim at Somerset Academy was out of the question. That meant no outlet for her restless energy and more time to get worked up about this date that wasn't a date.

Too keyed up to sit around her apartment, she arrived early at the Golden Dragon restaurant on Depot Street only to discover a sign on the door saying they were closed due to the power outage.

Disappointment was a hollow pit in her stomach. It took a lot of nerve for her to invite a man out. They often felt the need to prove themselves to her, because she was a judge and successful in her own right. Glen Plankey was single, intelligent, and seemed confident except for public speaking. It had been a big jump for her to ask him out. She didn't want the last two nights of tossing and turning to be for nothing.

Yet even if they never shared a meal together, seeing him today was worth every second of lost sleep.

He pulled into the parking spot beside her in a dark BMW and got out of the driver's side. His lean physique in a black, quilted down jacket and snug denim jeans would be the new feature in her late-night fantasies.

She wanted to run her fingers through his trim dark beard and get lost in his aquamarine eyes, glittering beneath thick brows and the edge of a navy pom beanie.

When she unrolled her window and he leaned down to speak to her, she read aloud the caption on his hat. "Good Vibes."

"Birthday present from my kids," he explained without embarrassment or apology.

"Nice."

Nodding to the restaurant door and the closed sign, he said, "Guess we won't have Chinese food after all."

No way was she letting him go without a fight. "There's another place if you're interested."

He shrugged. "As long as it's not too far away. I have to get the kids tonight, and it's a six-hour drive home in good weather."

"It will only take a few minutes to get there. We can take my car."

"Sounds good. Just let me turn mine off."

While he saw to his vehicle, she hastily scooped up the files and notebooks on the front passenger seat and tossed them into the back. Her SUV was like a mobile office, always filled with papers, maps, and other legal paraphernalia. She left the planning board materials in the back seat year-round. No one ever rode in it, so she had no reason to clean it out.

Once he was settled in the front seat, she reversed out of the parking lot and left Depot Street for Gore Mountain. The plow trucks had made one pass up the steep, winding road, forging little more than a tunnel between tall snowbanks on either side. Branches, white and heavy laden, stretched across the gap above them like fingers reaching for one another.

"Hopefully we won't meet anyone coming down," she said.

"I didn't know there were any restaurants up here. Except for The Gables."

"That's where we're going."

Abby concentrated on the road ahead, keeping her speed steady to avoid spinning and possibly going into a slide. Outside, the world was a white hush; inside the car was quiet as well. In good weather she would start a conversation, but right now she appreciated the silence.

A few minutes later they topped a foothill and came to a stop before Somerset Gables. The stately, three-storied building with white clapboards and green roofs presided over a breathtaking view of

Kingdom Lake and the surrounding mountains. Today it sat glistening beneath the pale winter sun, frosted with snow like an old-fashioned Christmas card.

"There aren't any cars here," he noted. "Are you sure they're serving?"

"They will be for me."

Raising his eyebrows, he said nothing, but got out of the car when she did and joined her on the walkway.

She noticed him reading the sign on the front door, which said the inn was closed for renovations.

"Trust me."

The door wasn't locked. Walking in, she grinned at him before calling out, "Honey, I'm home!"

Clattering noises came from behind white batwing doors to their left, followed by the sound of approaching footsteps. Then her favorite Chinese man frowned over the top of the doors at them. "Do you know how much snow we got last night?"

She was expecting this. Deliberately provoking him, she said, "No, but if I had to guess I'd say eleven or twelve inches."

"Yet you drove up the hill in it anyway?"

"Don't be a nag. The Golden Dragon lost power, and I'm in the mood for some ethnic food. Your ethnicity, that is."

Shaking his head, he pushed the doors apart and stepped into the lobby, wrapping both arms around her middle and hoisting her a few inches into the air to plant a kiss on her cheek. "Someone has to tell you when you're not being your usual logical self, little sister."

"I'm older than you," she grinned. They'd been over this more than once.

Putting her back on her feet, he kept one arm loosely draped around her middle. "I'm still bigger." With another kiss to the top of her head, he turned his attention to Glen. "Who is this?"

This is the man of my dreams. Literally. But as excited as she was about this lunch date, she managed to keep that answer to herself. "This is my neighbor. Glen, this is my brother David Wang. David, meet Glen Plankey."

Her brother extended his hand and Glen shook it, two good-looking men taking one another's measure. "Plankey? Are you related to the owner of the Town Line Diner?"

"Linda's my sister."

"Oh! That's why she looked so familiar at the wedding," Abby realized.

David raised his eyebrows. "You didn't get married and forget to tell me, did you?"

"Very funny." Ducking out of his hold, she kicked off her boots and put them on the mat beside the door. "You know when I get married, you'll be the one giving me away."

"Gladly," he teased. "Can't wait to get rid of you."

"*Wǒ yě ài nǐ.*" Abby moved to the coat rack and unbuttoned her jacket.

"*Tíngzhǐ.* Glen will think we're trading state secrets or something."

"Or something." To Glen she asked, "Can I take your coat?"

He unzipped his parka and handed it over, then toed off his boots, placing them next to hers. She admired the way his red, zip-front fleece caressed his long spine and stretched across the breadth of his chest. Just for a moment she wanted to rub against him, to see if she had imagined how perfectly her head fit into the notch between his pecs the other night.

Instead, she kept her distance, and when they were

both in stocking feet, they followed David through the batwing doors. On the other side was a deep room with two coolers at the end and a spotless steel worktop in the middle, a typical restaurant kitchen.

"So, what'll it be?" David asked.

"What have you got? I can help."

"Not a chance." He pulled a chef's shirt from a nail beside the doors and slipped it on over the T-shirt he wore.

"Hey! I'm brilliant in the kitchen."

"Well, you are brilliant. A brilliant slob, that is." To Glen he said, "Have you seen her condo?"

He shrugged. "A little bit."

David looked horrified. "You actually let a man into that place?"

"Hey, I clean!" Abby could feel her cheeks heat with embarrassment. Her condo wasn't *that* bad. "As a matter of fact, I was up cleaning half the night Friday."

"You must have been worried about something, then." David pulled a bag of rice noodles from a refrigerator. "Or excited." He raised his eyebrows in question, waiting for her to explain. Her cheeks grew even hotter. Avoiding eye contact with both men, she hoped her brother would drop the subject, but he didn't get the hint. "Ahh." He looked from her to Glen. "I see, said the very wise Chinaman."

Time for the direct approach. "Be quiet or I'll help you whether you want it or not."

"That sounds like a serious threat," a new voice interjected, coming from the tall, dark-skinned man who ducked beneath the lintel to enter from the lobby. He smiled and his face radiated joy, all of it directed at her. "You wouldn't be thinking of dirtying his sacred domain, would you, little sister?"

"You know it, baby brother."

The words were barely out of her mouth before he picked her up like a small child and gave her a loud kiss on the cheek, then deposited her back on her feet again. "Last time I checked, your mother's son was six months younger than me. That makes him the baby brother." He offered his hand to Glen. "I'm Romney Wilson."

"Glen Plankey."

Romney moved past the steel worktop and into the walk-in cooler. A moment later he popped his head out, asking, "Wet or dry stir-fry?"

"Wet," Abby said. "Dry," David answered at the exact same time.

Looking at Glen, her younger brother asked, "What do you think?"

"I don't know the difference."

"Well, do you prefer fish or beef?"

Holding his hands up in an *I surrender* motion, he said, "Whatever Abby wants."

Romney smiled at his answer. "Smart man."

David groaned. "That's it, then." Taking a wok from a hook above his head, he pointed it at Abby. "You take care of the fish."

"Bossy," Romney said, emerging from the walk-in with bok choy in one hand and scallions in the other.

"She likes bossy men."

Abby didn't miss the speculative look that crossed Glen's face, but all he said was, "What can I do?"

"Can you cook?" Romney asked.

"My kids don't complain much."

Both brothers stopped moving. She could just see them re-evaluating her guest and knew his worth had doubled in their eyes with that answer.

"You're a father," David finally said. "Congratulations."

"Well, I've had them for a while. They're teenagers."

"Condolences." This from Romney, but it lightened the mood, and everyone went back into action. "Here, you can come around and wash the vegetables for me while I get the fish out of the walk-in."

David oiled the wok and put it over a burner. Glen worked at the prep sink. Romney returned with an armload of seafood ingredients, putting them down to take something from a high shelf. "Here, little sister, I have a new puzzle for you."

"Awesome." It was one of those metal, mind-bender things that people give as Christmas gifts.

She loved them and her brothers knew it. Leaning against the counter, she studied the links and their pattern for a few minutes, made a twist here, a turn there, and solved the puzzle.

"Damn, that was fast, even for you."

"I'm impressed," Glen smiled. He was chopping scallions into little pieces on a fiberglass cutting board.

"You ever try those things?" Romney asked him.

"I've done a few."

"Here." He took a different puzzle down from the same shelf and handed it to Glen.

He solved the puzzle in seconds.

"Double damn. I think he beat Abby's time on that one."

"Now I'm impressed," she admitted.

David clapped his hands. "None of this will put food in your belly. C'mon, people. I need fish!"

The affectionate bickering continued throughout their meal preparation. She hoped Glen wasn't put off by it. He seemed to be enjoying the repartee even if he didn't say much.

****

Glen was having a great time.

It was a relief to watch Abby with her brothers and find that he enjoyed her company.

That he lusted after her was never in question. He had from the moment he saw her at the wedding and despised himself for it, so when she made the comment about her black blood, it was just what he needed. It let him channel his passion into safer emotions. Anger. Revulsion. They protected him against baser feelings. But on Friday night he'd lost that armor, and it sent him into a tailspin. He wanted to sleep with a woman he knew nothing about. That kind of mindless desire was foreign to him. Even in his adolescence he couldn't remember anything this powerful.

When she removed her coat in the lobby, he'd considered helping her, but he couldn't trust himself to touch her in front of an audience. And he badly wanted to touch her, especially with that ivory sweater clinging to her form like it had been knitted on. Then there were the brown tweed pants, molded to her backside before flaring out and elongating her legs. Imagining what she looked like beneath them almost robbed him of the ability to speak.

Now she was shucking scallops like a pro, a job he would never want, while bantering with her brothers. All three treated him more like a familiar face than a first-time guest.

"Glen, can you hand me the pickled chilies?" This from David. "They're up over your head. Or my head. For you they're at eye level."

"How's it feel to be shorter than everyone around you?" Abby smirked.

"Keep it up, and I'll make you peel garlic cloves." To Glen he added, "She hates garlic."

"The taste is bad enough." She wrinkled her nose. "How do you ever get the smell off your hands?"

"Wash them?"

"Very funny. Don't listen to anything he says about my cleaning or my personal hygiene."

"She's just a paper freak, really," Romney explained. "Stacks and stacks of it everywhere." With his hands he indicated a two-foot pile and another and another. "What about you, Glen? What do you do when you're not being put to work in a kitchen?"

"I'm in the securities industry."

"That's a broad answer. What, exactly, is your role?"

"Provide security for securities. I'm a tech guy; I help prevent hackers and viruses from bringing the whole market down."

Both brothers paused and looked at Abby, who studiously avoided eye contact.

"So, you're a geek?" Romney finally asked.

"Guilty."

"Me too," Romney admitted. "A coder."

David, with a speculative gleam in his dark eyes, said, "Ahhh, I see, said the wise Chinaman."

"*Tíngzhǐ*," Abby muttered.

"Don't mind them," Romney said. "Abby's the one who turned me on to languages. That's her specialty."

This was interesting. Another layer to the little judge. "You code?"

The brothers burst out laughing at his question. Abby's cheeks turned pink but she answered him. "No. I have a thing for languages, though. When Romney was a boy, I tried teaching him patterns in languages, and that's how he got started."

"What's so funny about that?" Glen wondered.

"She hates technology," David explained.

"I don't hate it. Not exactly."

"Did you change the clock in your car when daylight savings began this year? Or when it ended?"

She shrugged. "What's the point? It only changes again six months later."

"Uh-huh. And what about your new television? Have you programmed the remote yet?"

Abby transferred the scallops to a plate beside her older brother, looking pleased with herself when she said, "As a matter of fact, my remote is programmed."

He didn't look impressed. Instead, he turned to Romney. "You did it for her?"

"Of course, I did it for her. She wouldn't let me touch her answering machine at the office, though."

"It still records messages as being on a different day?"

"It's two days, nine hours less six minutes off." Her tone was defensive.

"While it could be, I don't know, current?"

Ignoring his sarcasm, she said, "There's nothing wrong with leaving it the way it is. I can add and subtract, you know. It *is* possible to tell when the messages come in."

Her brothers laughed again, and Glen was tempted to join them. Knowing this bright, successful woman had idiosyncrasies to her personality just made her more interesting. By the time they washed their hands and sat at a long table near the windows for their meal, he realized this was the best date he'd had in years. Maybe ever.

"You're probably wondering about the whole brother-sister thing," Romney said.

"*Tíngzhǐ*," David admonished. "Eat. Don't talk."

"Are you sure you're full-blood Chinese? We eat with our mouths open. We talk at the table."

They did. Glen's quick mind had no trouble keeping up with the running conversation, but it was fast and sometimes bounced randomly from subject to subject. Abby was the quietest of the three. She inserted a word here or there, sometimes in English, sometimes in Chinese, interrupting once to tell her brothers that Glen had a tight schedule and couldn't spend all day listening to them. That naturally led to questions about his kids, where he lived, and why he decided to make a weekend home of Jason's abandoned condo.

By the time they stood in the lobby putting on their coats and boots, he could tell he had passed her brothers' litmus test. They shook his hand warmly, squeezed her to within an inch of her life, and waved them off at the door. "*Wǒ ài nǐ*," Abby called as she rounded the hood of her car.

"*Wǒ yě ài nǐ*," they chorused back at her.

Then the two of them were cocooned in the frosted automobile, the heater working to clear the windows before they could leave the parking lot. She looked a little embarrassed and tilted her head a couple of times like she was about to say something but didn't, so he broke the ice for her.

"What does shu-shu mean?"

"Shusha?"

"I figured *tíngzhǐ* means cut it out or something like that."

"It means stop."

"But you also said shu-shu a lot. I couldn't tell if it was one or two words."

"Oh!" Gray-green eyes rounded with understanding. "*Xie xie.* That's thank you."

"Ah. And *wǒ yě ài nǐ*?"

Abby turned the wiper blades on. They cleared the windshield enough for her to see, and she backed out of the yard before replying. "It means, I love you too."

He didn't ask any other questions, instead letting her focus on descending the steep S curves toward town while he enjoyed being in the car with her.

He liked her. In one lunch hour he had learned more about her than he probably would have over several dates, and each new discovery made him want to know more.

"Thank you for lunch," he said when they arrived at the Golden Dragon parking lot.

"You're welcome." She looked at his BMW, crusted over with frost. "Do you want me to wait while you warm your car up?"

"Sure." He hit the remote start button on his key fob and watched to make sure the running lights came on before turning back to face her. "I like your brothers."

She smiled, affection in her tone when she spoke. "They're the best. Even if they can be a pain."

"Something tells me you don't mind all that much."

"Not really."

"At the risk of sounding racist again, can you explain your family tree?"

She laughed and he liked the sound of it. "I wondered when you might ask about that. My father and mother split up when I was little. She's white. He's half white, half black, and all Bahamian. After that he moved in with a Chinese American woman who had a little boy. David. Two and a half years later they had Romney together. Six months after that my mother had a son, Hume. His last name's Kelly."

"Are you close with him too?"

"Love him to pieces."

He would not have expected any other answer. He might have asked more, but a plow truck lumbered across the parking lot behind them and disturbed the moment.

"We should probably get our cars out of here for him to clean up," she said, reluctance clear in her voice.

He didn't want to leave her either. "Can I get your phone number?"

"My number?" Her gray-green eyes lit up at his question.

"The policewoman suggested we exchange numbers. So I can check on you, because of the creeper."

"Oh." He didn't miss the way her eyes dimmed at the explanation or the disappointment in her voice, but she quickly ducked her head to retrieve a cell phone from her purse where it sat between their seats.

Waiting until she turned the screen on and looked at him again, he added, "And so I can call you."

Little white teeth bit into her soft lower lip.

He wanted to lave the indenture with his tongue. Instead, he took her phone, sent a text to himself, and gave it back to her. "There. Now my number is stored in your memory, and I've got yours."

She put the phone back in her purse. The plow truck made another pass behind them. Time was running out for both of them.

"I'm going to kiss you, Abby."

"Uh-huh."

He loved the way she didn't hesitate with her response, though her face flushed, and the pulse at the side of her neck started racing.

It was a hard, dry kiss. Not satisfying by a long shot, but he didn't want to presume any more than he already had. He could still remember the shock in her eyes fifteen years ago when his ex-wife made him sound like an animal. He didn't want to scare her away.

So, his heart skipped a beat when she whispered, "More. Please."

Nothing turned him on quite like a woman who knew what she wanted and wasn't afraid to ask for it. Except maybe this woman. Everything about her excited him. Grasping her shoulders and pulling her close, he slid his tongue along the seam of her lips until they opened, then delved into the warm recess of her mouth.

She met him with equal passion, and when her fingers slid beneath the brim of his hat, scraping the sides of his skull with her nails, a sizzle raced up his spine. He was a teenage boy again. On fire with lust for her like it was the first time he ever held a woman; he was ready to put the car seats back and fog up the windows.

The plow truck made a third pass across the parking lot.

Chapter Four

"I like the way Chinese tastes on you."

Abby could still hear those parting words. She pictured his lips, glistening from their kiss, beckoning her to come back for more, and oh, how she wanted to. But he had a long drive to make, children to take care of, and they were parked in the way of the plow truck operator. So she said a reluctant goodbye and drove back to their building alone.

The first floor housed a laundromat and hair salon, both closed today. The second floor held professional offices, including her law firm, a CPA, and a dentist. No cars were in the lot when she arrived and none when she looked out the hall window half an hour later.

Darn. He must have left for New York directly from the Golden Dragon. That meant no chance of another kiss.

She moped back to her condo and might have spent her whole night feeling sorry for herself if Jason hadn't called to check on her. When she assured him that she was okay, he warned her that whoever the predator was, he liked redheaded women best. Her hair color was chestnut. Technically that was brown with a red hue, but he advised her to take extra precautions.

"I will," she assured him. "But thanks for the call. It's kind of weird being here by myself now that you've moved out."

She wasn't fishing. Really. Yet her heart skipped a beat at his answer. "Glen was sorry he couldn't stay longer."

"He was?" For the second time that weekend, her toes curled. Knowing he discussed her with his best friend made her giddy.

"He said to tell you he looks forward to a longer stay next time."

Just like that her mood changed. She floated through mundane household chores, made an elaborate meal of tossed salad and grilled tilapia, even adding a sprig of parsley to the lemon wedge on the plate, and put enough bubble bath in the tub to fill a swimming pool.

Propping her phone up on the back of the commode where she could reach it, she slid into the frothy water. Judge Henry liked to call on Sunday nights and discuss her upcoming week. If she didn't hear from him by eight o'clock, it meant he had gone to bed early or lost phone service due to the storm. He had a landline because he didn't believe in cell phones; like he had a live-in housekeeper who saw to all his needs because he didn't believe in marriage.

When the digital display read five past the hour, she sank beneath the water line and stretched her limbs. Since she had been unable to swim today, this was the next best thing.

The phone rang.

Emerging with a sputter, bubbles flying in every direction, she blinked to clear the water from her eyes but couldn't read the number of the incoming call. She answered just in case it was important, but annoyance at having her relaxation disturbed showed in her testy greeting. "Who is this?"

A brief hesitation. "Abby? It's Glen."

She groaned, wanting to sink below the surface again. "Sorry about that. I couldn't see who it was and figured it was a junk call."

"I think I should be apologizing to you. It sounds like you're busy."

"What? No! I'm just in the tub." Why had she told him that? Now he was sure to end the call. "Really. It's fine. I'm fine."

"Hmmm." His voice dropped down suggestively. "I don't suppose you'd like to send a picture to prove it?"

Abby sucked in a surprised breath. Had her fantasy man just said those words to her? Below the water line she clenched her knees together. Suddenly the temperature seemed warmer than it had been. A catch in her voice betrayed her reaction. "I don't know how."

"Good. I wasn't serious."

"Oh. Of course." Mortified, she wanted to dive below the bubbles and not come up until tomorrow. "Sorry, I didn't mean—"

"Don't apologize. I was teasing. But once your image is out there in cyberspace, you can't ever take it back. I'm glad you don't know how."

Better to be thought a fool than to open your mouth and remove all doubt. That saying kept her silent now. She had never felt more like a fool.

"I told Jason I'd check in with you each night, so he doesn't have to. Unless your brothers are already planning to?"

"No." David was still working between his Manchester restaurant and The Gables. He probably didn't even know about the creeper. Romney was only here for the weekend.

"Then I'll make the calls."

Just like that he was taking charge of her safety. Pretty presumptuous for someone she barely knew, even if he could kiss like his life depended on it. But did she want him to be this involved in her life? Yes! Definitely.

"We should have a code, though."

"A code?" Great. First, she sounded like a naïve teenager, now a parrot. Her usual cool head must be buried beneath the bubbles somewhere. "What do you have in mind?"

"Well, if someone is there and I ask you how you are, you might say you're okay even though you're not. So, what if when I call, you tell me what time it is?"

"Umm, all right." It seemed to her that a genius could come up with something more original, so she said, "Isn't that kind of simple?"

"Not if your answer is two days, nine hours less six minutes off."

Stunned he had paid that much attention to the silly banter between her and her brothers, she tried not to read too much into it. "I can't believe you remember that."

"I remember everything." His voice dropped down low, creating an intimacy between them that transcended distance. "Especially what happened in the car."

She squeezed her eyes closed tight to contain her reaction when what she wanted was to squeal like a schoolgirl.

"I only wish it could have lasted longer," he added.

"Me too."

"Dad, have you seen my charger?" a high-pitched, young voice interrupted.

"Isn't it on your dresser?"

"No! Colin used it last, and he said he put it back, but I can't find it."

A young, male voice in the background said something, and an argument was on.

"Sunday nights are so much fun," Glen said on a long-suffering sigh. "Looks like I have to go now, but I'll call again tomorrow night."

Just when it was getting good, too. "Okay."

"Abby? I don't want you putting yourself at risk, but I would have loved that picture."

****

She loved the way he said goodbye. Each night he ended their conversation with something provocative. It didn't matter if they talked for three minutes or twenty. When they disconnected, she was more excited than when she first took his call. And that was saying something.

She slept better than ever and hardly slept at all. In the mornings she dove into the pool with more energy than she had ever had, the water sluicing over her skin waking up nerve endings she didn't even know were dormant. Everything she ate tasted like ambrosia, yet she had almost no appetite. Temperatures dropped midweek, and a wintry mix left the Northeast Kingdom slick with ice, but she stood on the balcony admiring the way the moon shone on the ice after the storm ended. When the sun melted away the top layer the next day, she stared out her office window at the dripping eaves and thought nothing had ever been quite so beautiful.

By Friday afternoon she was ready to pinch herself.

Moving to Somerset had been a gamble. She had dreamed of someday settling in Vermont's Northeast Kingdom, but it had been a distant, sometime-in-the-future kind of ambition. Maybe when she made partner. Or got married. Or things slowed down a little.

Then Judge Henry recommended her to replace a retiring judge in Essex County's civil court division. She would sit on the bench in the same courtroom in Guildhall where she had clerked for him all those years ago. Where, as a doe-eyed twenty-year-old with no experience of men, she had witnessed the dissolution of Glen Plankey's marriage and revelations of a sex life that had dominated her fantasies ever since.

Of course, her mother objected to her accepting the post even as she bragged to her friends about the offer. She said Abby was crazy to consider it and would miss the city. That her career would come to a standstill. There were about three hundred people total in the town of Guildhall, not even redeemed by a view unless she wanted to stare out the window at the non-existent traffic.

And what would she do with the rest of her days? Court was in session about once a month. How would she make a living? Where would she live? The largest nearby town was across the river in New Hampshire; Lancaster, and certainly no metropolis.

Abby tried explaining that she wasn't exactly *living* in Rutland. Most of her days began at sunup and didn't end until the stroke of midnight. She fell into bed at night exhausted, only to wake and do it again. On the rare occasions when she wasn't answering emails, listening to voicemails, or proofreading volumes of legal documents that clients never read, she could barely function at all. That was the problem when life was moving at full speed ahead. The moment it stopped, it stopped completely.

She was miserable. Her girlish dreams of marriage and family were slipping further and further from her grasp. She could understand Judge Henry's cynicism, and even though she didn't share it, she was afraid some day she would end up like him. Alone.

When the opportunity came to take over a small law practice in Somerset, she jumped on it. The town was halfway between Guildhall and Rutland in size. It had a quarry mine, a lumber yard, and a collection of small businesses primarily run as sole proprietorships. Farms sprawled from the downtown area to the south and west, forest to the north and east. The people were honest, hardworking, reserved, and mostly self-sufficient, and the favorable ratio of men to women was one of its biggest attractions for her.

If she was lucky, she might just meet a man like the one in the courtroom all those years ago. She'd never dreamed of seeing the man himself.

****

Glen took the kids out for supper on Friday night before taking them to his ex-wife's house. It was a ritual for them, but it meant he didn't get home until almost ten o'clock. He had to wait much longer than he wished to before hearing the sexy, little judge's voice on his phone.

She picked up on the second ring. "Hello, Glen."

"Sorry I'm late. I hope you're safe and sound inside your condo."

They both knew if she were in danger, there was nothing he could do from New York City, but neither one of them said it.

"I'm good. That is, for six past one on a Wednesday afternoon."

"Glad to hear it. That means you'll be up for hours still."

She laughed, and he sank into his oversized easy chair, kicking off his shoes and staring at the dark ceiling. He hadn't even turned on the living room lights when he got home. Talking to her was more important. "Jason tells me you don't sleep on Friday nights, anyway."

"Eventually I do. It just takes a while to unwind."

He wished he could be there to help her relax. Just thinking about her reaction to his nearness, when he pressed her against the wall and told her to remove his cuffs, could raise his blood pressure. He tried not to think of the kiss at all. A man could only take so much excitement and still hold onto his sanity.

"Do you play chess, Abby?"

"As a matter of fact, I do."

Deliberately lowering his voice because he knew she liked it, he said, "Will you play with me?"

Her breathing was loud in his ear. Like a favorite symphony, the sound rippled through his mind and spread out through his body, making him lean back in his chair and stretch to accommodate the sensation. He flipped the footrest up and let his head fall back against the padded cushion.

"Is that a yes?"

"I'd love to be your playmate," she whispered.

Glen groaned out loud. She was a quick study. After the first night's call, he had been using sexual innuendos as a form of telephone foreplay because a six-hour drive lay between them and prevented the real thing. By midweek she had mastered the art.

"Let's get started then."

Hours later the game ended in a draw. He put away his chess board, where he had been making both his own moves and moves for her, and since she had yawned twice in the last thirty minutes, he thought they would end the call, but she surprised him.

"I want you to know that I remembered you."

What was this?

"I mean, I remember you from that day at the courthouse in Guildhall."

Oh.

Part of him was glad she brought it out into the open while another part of him didn't know if he was ready to go there yet. They had a mutual attraction and so far, a harmless flirtation. He liked that she was a career woman whose brain matched her body. He wanted to know more about both. If they discussed his downfall before the judge, what they had could be ruined before it even had a chance to grow.

"Did you remember me?" she asked when he didn't speak for several moments.

Should he tell her? Did he want her to know how much he'd resented her presence that day? How, in a twisted way, she had come to symbolize everything he lost?

Instead of a direct answer, he said, "The things my ex-wife told the judge..."

"Were they true?"

There was truth and then there was truth, mere shades apart depending on the situation, the audience, perceptions. He didn't know how much truth she could handle. "Would you like me more or less if they were?"

Silence. He had to know the answer to the question before he could trust her with anything more.

"Abby? I'm too old to play games, and I don't want to mislead you."

"Then be honest with me, and I'll do the same."

Glen sat up in his chair and flipped down the footrest. This could be a big mistake. "I haven't slept with a woman in almost two years." And none of them had known anything about him that he didn't want to share. She already knew more than most.

"Slept?"

"Slept with one *or* slept in bed with one."

"And before that?"

"I had a few relationships. Most of them were over in three or four months."

At first his ex-wife had tried to sabotage every relationship. She didn't want him to be happy with anyone else because she simply didn't want to see him happy. He'd stopped dating for years and only started again when the kids were old enough to know it was normal.

"And now?"

"Now I'm ready for a mature woman. One who knows what she wants and wants me for myself. Not my income or what I can provide."

He had a feeling she could be that woman.

Abby's voice was low when she spoke next. "Did she tell the truth about your sexual preferences? About how often you like it, or how you like it?"

The direct question forced him to be vulnerable with her. "I'm afraid to answer that question."

"The world has changed a lot in fifteen years. People don't look at things like that the same way anymore."

She knew how long it had been. He didn't dare read too much into it, though. This was the same woman who knew what time it was two days, nine hours less six minutes in the past. He jumped restlessly up from his chair and paced the length of the dark living room. "I don't care what people think. Only what you do."

"Then I hope it's true."

That breathy comment ensured he was in a state of semi-arousal for the rest of the weekend and all the following week. Their nightly phone calls were sweet torture. He didn't know what her condo looked like, but he could imagine her sprawled across a sofa, only her tiny feet and hands visible while the rest of her body was swathed in pink fleece. Soft fabric that had intimate knowledge of golden curves he wanted the right to.

By the time he left New York City on Friday afternoon, his nerves were shot, and it showed.

"Geez, Dad, don't bite my head off. I was only asking if we could stop for supper somewhere," Darcy complained.

"I don't usually take her side, but we do need to eat," Colin chipped in. "And you know she'll get carsick if she has to go without food for too long."

True. His daughter, almost fifteen, was having trouble regulating her blood sugar. The doctors thought her thyroid was the problem, but until they finished analyzing her blood work, she was supposed to eat every three hours to keep it level.

"Sorry, guys." He didn't usually neglect something that important, and his kids knew it. "Just let me get north of Hartford, and then we'll stop."

But even in Windsor his thoughts turned to Abby. How could they not when the kids chose to eat at a Chinese restaurant?

"You got something on your mind, Dad?" Colin asked after they placed their order.

"What? No."

"More like *someone*, I think," Darcy offered.

Glen wrapped an arm around her neck and knuckled the top of her perceptive little head. "Don't be a brat."

Unperturbed, she pulled out of his embrace and leaned back against the banquet seating, patting her hair into place. Once the soft, brown curls were rearranged to her liking, she turned wide, blue eyes on him. The picture of youthful innocence. The image was spoiled when she smirked at her brother and said, "See? Told you so."

For the remainder of the trip, they were either harassing him about his alleged preoccupation or bickering over the music choice on the radio. Their constant noise mixed with the stress of the long trip and two weeks of nervous anticipation finally got the best of him until he demanded, "Haven't you two ever heard of a nap?"

"Nope," Colin answered. "This is our way of keeping you awake."

"I've never fallen asleep at the wheel before."

"Well, there's always a first time, with you being so old and all."

"He's not old," Darcy argued.

"Thank you."

"But he's getting there," she added.

"See?" As if his sister had justified his own observations.

Smug little brats.

"Really, Dad, you should start thinking about retirement. You know, maybe getting away from the city, slowing down a little bit."

Glen knew exactly where this was going. His kids lived in Scarsdale, rural to many of his co-workers and friends but not to them. Nothing meant country to these two like Vermont's Northeast Kingdom. When they were little, they would pester him about when they were making the next trip up to see his family. They forgot the hours it took to get there. They overlooked the fact that Darcy regularly got carsick several times during the journey.

"She has a point, Dad."

"Uh-huh. And how would I see you if I did that?"

"We could come with you," Darcy exclaimed, and he knew at once he had been set up for this assault. Walked right into it because he was thinking about a luscious, little body when he should have been giving the kids his full attention. "Just consider it. I could get a job with Aunt Linda at the diner. Colin could help on the farm."

"And what would I do?"

"I don't know. There must be a company there that needs a computer guy. Maybe a bank."

Although she didn't realize it, his daughter had ripped the scab off a fifteen-year-old wound, and despite the passage of time, it left him raw and bloody inside.

A month after getting his degree, he had returned home to Somerset and took a job managing the local Community National Bank branch. He loved it. Despite his fear of public speaking, he was good at talking to customers. He understood farmers and small business owners. Enjoyed working with people he had known all his life, those same people who had raised money for scholarship programs like the ones that helped send him to a second-tier college for a first-class education. He joined the Rotary Club and took a seat on the Chamber of Commerce. Played basketball once a week with Jason and the other guys from their high school team.

There was only one problem. Jillian hated everything. She hated his job, the town of Somerset, and the people in it. She had expected more from him when she met him during his sophomore year of college and seduced him a few months later. And it was a seduction. It hadn't taken him long to realize that right from their first meeting, she set her sights on having him. She thought she was landing a future paycheck with the added benefit of it looking good on her arm. The last thing she expected was for him to move back to his childhood home, where cows outnumbered people, and nothing was open past eight o'clock at night.

Just as effectively as she had seduced him into an "accidental" pregnancy and marriage before he was even done with his degree, she set out to sabotage his new life. As far as she was concerned, he owed her more than that. Felt she deserved more.

"Earth to Dad?" Colin sing-songed from the front passenger seat.

Glen shook himself back to the present. "What?"

"You missed the Lyndonville exit. Are we getting off in Lyndon or going all the way to Newport?"

"I guess we're getting off in Lyndon."

"Want me to drive for you?"

"No, I'm good." Then he softened the rejection. "I'll let you get some driving in this weekend."

"Told you he has a woman on his mind."

Chapter Five

Abby would be lying if she said she hadn't been waiting to hear the elevator swish. She left her door open most of the night so she wouldn't miss it, but when the grandfather clock in the corner of the living room chimed two in the morning, she accepted that something must have happened to change his plans. She closed and locked the door.

It was too late for a bath, so she tossed her thick hair into a loose topknot and made do with a short steam facial. Applied a generous application of night cream to her face, neck, and shoulders. Then, because that felt so good, she slipped out of her fleece robe and took a scented body lotion from the cabinet that Romney had given her after one of his European trips. Starting with her toes, she rubbed it into every inch of exposed skin. Moved on to her ankles. By the time she finished with her calves and reached the tender spot at the back of her knees, she was relaxed to the point of bonelessness.

Naturally thoughts of Glen Plankey slipped into the humid atmosphere. When she smoothed lotion into her thighs, she wished it was his hands kneading the muscles. Her fingers skimmed dangerously close to a place that no man had ever satisfied. He could.

Fifteen years ago, she hadn't known fulfillment would be so hard to achieve. Then she had some sexual experiences of her own and knew the disappointment that came with every one. Eventually she'd found release in the same way women had been finding it for centuries. By imagining someone else was in bed with her. A man whose name she couldn't remember but whose face was imprinted on her brain; dark hair, blue eyes, and an innate dignity radiating from him even while his life was torn to shreds on the courtroom floor.

Now that image had matured. Taken on a name. Instead of a stranger dominating her late-night fantasies, it was a real man. One with a quick smile, a demanding job, teenage children, and a penchant for dirty telephone talk.

Just as she slid lotion-filled hands over the tips of her breasts, the phone rang.

She squawked.

Feeling as if she had been caught in the act of touching herself, she snatched up a thin dressing gown and wrapped it around her body before plucking her cell phone from the counter. It was two thirty in the morning. It was Glen.

"Hello." Her greeting was breathless, excited, exactly the way she felt.

"Hi, yourself. Did I catch you in the tub again?"

"No."

"But you're okay? You sound a little...rushed."

"I'm fine. Now."

"Show me."

Abby was confused. He said photographing herself wasn't a good idea. "How do I do that?"

"Come to your terrace door and I'll come to mine."

He was here! She almost spun around in circles, so thrilled to hear his voice and know he was in the same building again. Instead, she clutched the phone to her chest and rushed into her bedroom. Was her racing heart loud enough for him to hear over their connection? Did she care?

She couldn't even pretend she wasn't desperate to see him again. Hear his voice. More.

Hurrying to pull the heavy drapes aside from the glass door, she hooked them so only the sheer curtain stood between her and the glass panel. A single lamp glowed from a table in the corner of the room. Across the snow-covered grillwork, his outside light was on, but she couldn't see into the interior of his unit.

"Are you there?"

He flicked the light twice. "Kids just crashed. I'm trying not to wake them." His voice was a whisper in her ear.

"Can you see me?"

"An outline. Do you have more light?"

Her thin robe gaped open at the neckline when she bent to turn on the second bedside lamp. The material was soft against her lotion-scented body. It wasn't his hands, but it felt good, and it gave her an idea. She returned to stand at the door but kept the sheer curtain in place. "Is this better?"

"You haven't convinced me yet."

Feeling completely decadent, she slipped the knot on the robe's tie and let it fall from her shoulders to pool at her feet. She knew the lamps would reveal her outline to him and although she wasn't vain, she also knew they would flatter her short hourglass figure.

"How is this?"

"Better." His voice was rough.

She came closer to the glass pane. Put her phone on speaker and lay it on a small shelf beside the door so she could take the filmy sheer in both hands and stroke it between her fingers. She gathered it until it was a few inches wide and lay it over one shoulder, then turned so that it wrapped around her body, covering her breasts, curling around the base of her spine and across one hip to fall in a pleated skirt at her feet.

"You look like a pinup goddess from another century."

She laughed, flattered, glad the image he saw was the same one she was going for.

"Is your hair in a bun?"

"Sort of."

"I can see ringlets all around the bottom."

She fingered a few curls with one hand while holding onto the sheer panel with the other. "I was in the bathroom. It was steamy."

"I want to lick the steam from your body."

Abby's tummy dipped. His voice was a throaty growl, and it vibrated through her. "That sounds...delicious."

"Every inch of it."

Emboldened by his reaction, she bent her knee at an angle and ran her toes up and down the opposite calf. His groan was loud in the room.

"If I was a dog I would be drooling right now."

Laughing, she stroked her hand down the length of the curtain then smoothed it between her inner thighs.

"Since I'm only a man, I'm willing to get on my knees and beg you for mercy."

Need stole the breath from her lungs. This little game was supposed to be for him, to tantalize him into wanting more, yet heat bubbled through her bloodstream. She pressed her body to the cool door panel but found no relief. She rolled her cheek against the frosted glass. "I've never had a man on his knees before."

The admission was a loud whisper filling the muted shadows of the room.

He didn't even pretend to misunderstand. Or miss the invitation. "Then I'll be the first."

"When?" Her voice caught, but she didn't care. "When can I see you?"

"What are you doing in the morning?"

"Swimming at Somerset Academy. Eight o'clock."

"I'll be there."

Abby dropped the sheer and stepped back from the glass door. Cool air was replaced by a sense of desolation. Her hand trembled when she took the phone from the shelf and turned off the speaker, bringing it to her ear. Unexpected tears gathered in her eyes, and she couldn't think of anything to say. She didn't want to let him go.

"Abby?"

His voice was soft, as if he understood the physical loss she was experiencing.

"Yes?"

Her limbs were shaking with need. When he spoke again, just three words, they filled the empty place inside her.

"I remember you."

****

Somerset Academy was a large brick building with wings added to either side sometime after it was built a century before. Back then it was simply called The Academy, but since the three gores officially merged to form a township just before Glen was born, it had been renamed. The old name and date of construction could still be found on the marble doorframe and etched into the granite steps of the main entrance.

He cut through the elementary school parking lot at the opposite end of the fifty-acre parcel shared by both schools and drove behind the academy building to the gym's back entrance. When he went there, it was a greenhouse. A few years ago, while renovating the adjacent science wing, the townspeople decided to replace it with an indoor swimming pool.

Abby was already in the pool. Despite the cap protecting her thick mane of chestnut hair, he could tell it was her tearing up the far lane with an impressive butterfly stroke. No one else had a figure like that. Last night he had committed every curve and hollow to memory, carrying the images into his dreams. He would never forget the alluring sight of her, cast in shadows by the lamps behind her, silhouetted against the balcony doors. He could find her in the dark. And he wanted to.

This morning she seemed to have a lot of energy to burn. When she reached the end of the lane where he stood, she flipped and vaulted away from him.

Glen stepped back and took a seat on one of the plastic lounge chairs lining this end of the pool apron.

She probably hadn't seen him. She probably didn't expect to, since he was well over half an hour late, but Darcy had been sick early this morning, and he couldn't leave until she was resting comfortably.

Then he'd hurried across town as fast as he could safely drive, not even stopping to warm the car up or scrape the windshield. Instead, he used the washer feature to wet the glass and the wipers to clear a space large enough to see where he was going while the defroster caught up.

There had been no reason to pack a swimsuit for the weekend. Even if he had, it would be too late to join her in the lanes, and he would have missed out on watching this display of what was, frankly, a very talented athlete in action.

He was a strong swimmer. Abby was a human torpedo, gliding through the water at top speed, then lunging to the surface for air before going under again.

At exactly nine o'clock she pulled herself out of the pool and swung her legs around on the concrete apron. Elbows on her knees, breaths choppy, thighs trembling, it took several minutes for her breathing to regulate, her chest to stop heaving and her stomach to stop hollowing out. At last, she stood and turned in his direction.

"Oh!"

Glen leapt to his feet and grabbed her before she fell backward into the pool.

Abby sputtered and clutched his forearms.

"Sorry. I didn't mean to startle you."

"It's okay." She regained her balance and put a hand to her chest as if trying to slow her heartrate. "I thought you hadn't come."

Glen resisted the urge to pull her closer. For the last two weeks they had been getting to know one another by telephone. They had worked themselves into a sexual frenzy, only to meet in a public place with people doing laps, children taking lessons at the shallow end of the pool, and a water aerobics class in progress on the other side.

"Are you ready to go?" he asked.

She disengaged herself from his hold and grabbed a towel from the end of a lounge chair. "I have to change first."

Another delay. More waiting before he could pick up where they left off in her car two weeks ago.

His disappointment must have shown, because she said, "I promise I'll be quick."

Pulling himself together, he looked at the clock on the wall then at an imaginary watch on his wrist. In his best imitation of a swim coach he warned, "I'm timing you."

A few minutes later she returned from the locker room dressed in a snug V-neck t-shirt over form-fitting yoga pants. Her hair lay like a thick, warm shawl around her shoulders, and he wanted to sink his fingers into the thick mass.

She had a winter coat in one hand and extended a duffel bag toward him with the other. "Can you hold this for me while I put my jacket on?"

Taking the handles of the blue nylon carryall, he didn't pay any attention to it until she had her coat on and took it back. That was when he noticed the word Colby emblazoned on the side below the white handles.

"No way." He laughed. "You're a lady mule."

"You know my school mascot? Did you go there?"

"Nope. I'm a Bobcat."

"What are the odds?" she smiled. "Me at Colby and you at Bates." The schools were notorious rivals.

"Small world. What was your major?"

"Classics. You?"

"Economics. You play any sports?"

"Swim team. It's the only form of exercise I enjoy." She pulled the edges of her coat together and tugged the zipper up over her ample bosom. "These things bounce all over the place and get in the way if I run or jump."

He kept his mouth shut, conscious of their surroundings, but he wasn't going to complain about her generous curves.

"I come here seven days a week. Usually for half an hour, but today I did double laps."

"Any special reason?"

She pulled gloves from her coat pocket and threaded them over her fingers. "I had some restless energy to burn."

Her smile left him with little doubt as to the cause.

"Sorry I'm late. Darcy was sick."

"Is she okay now?"

By unspoken agreement they started walking toward the exit. "Better."

"Good. How about you?" she prompted. "Did you play a sport in college?"

"Basketball. I still play two or three nights a week." He held the first set of doors open for her to pass through. "It's not the same as playing at Alumni Gym, but a few of the guys in New York are Batesies too."

"We even let in other members of the BBC once in a while," he grinned, referring to the acronym for Maine's competitive trio: Bates, Bowdoin, and Colby.

"How big of you."

He held the second set of doors, and they stepped out into a cold, clear day where the sun made crystals of the snow's crusty top layer. "Where to now?"

"I usually get a cinnamon tea from The Common Store."

"I'll follow you."

Downtown was busy, but they found side-by-side parking spots on the common and walked across the street to the general store.

Stepping inside was like entering a time warp for Glen. Plow truck operators mixed with people making their weekly dump runs, and retirees hung out at round tables by the window to watch passersby.

Some of the names and faces had changed over the last fifteen years, but there were enough similarities that it always felt like home.

Abby led the way to the coffee counter. The words *one size, one price, any flavor combination* were written in bold, pink letters above the list of choices on a chalkboard hanging behind the workers' station.

"I've seen your sister in here," she said while they waited their turn. It was a question, since Linda owned the diner and could get a cup of coffee any time she wanted to.

"I think she buys a special blend here and serves it at the restaurant."

A teenage girl introduced herself as Molly and asked what she could get for them.

"You know my answer." Turning to Glen, Abby said, "I come here every Saturday. Everybody knows my order. What would you like? My treat."

A few minutes later he had a regular coffee, and she had her cinnamon tea. "I usually sit in the corner," Abby said, dropping a dollar bill in the tip jar. She didn't move in the direction she had indicated, though, instead looking furtively around before stretching on her toes to whisper, "But do you really want to sit here and pretend we're not dying to touch each other?"

***

Glen's inhale was sharp, the need on his face instant and honest.

"No." His gravelly reply was proof, if she needed any, that they were on the same page.

"Follow me," Abby said. She wished she could take his free hand, but this was a public place, and she had a reputation to protect.

"I feel like a teenager," she admitted when they reached their vehicles. "Sneaking away to make out."

"Sounds like an invitation to me."

A sizzle ran up her spine. "Race you home."

Minutes later they parked in the lot outside their building and took the elevator up to the third floor. Abby sucked nervously at her tea. She wanted this, but she also wanted it to be as good as her imagination told her it could be and she didn't want to disappoint him.

The car came to a stop. Doors slid open. They crossed the square hall to her unit without speaking, and she entered the security code, then stepped inside the condo and stopped.

There was the wall; the place where Glen had been handcuffed but not helpless. Where she was protected by a policewoman only yards away but lost to his sensual assault.

The gleam in his blue eyes told her he was reliving those same memories.

"Put your tea down," he said in a tone that brooked no argument.

Cautiously she placed her to-go cup on the floor beside the welcome mat.

"Take off your coat."

He was already unzipping his and toeing off his boots. After doing the same, she hung their jackets on pegs beside the door. Her arms were stretched above her, back turned to him, when she felt the heat of his body at her back.

He circled her wrists with his hands. His breath was warm at her ear. "We have some unfinished business."

Abby closed her eyes and let her head fall back against his chest.

"I was frisked by that woman," Glen murmured. "Here. That night."

"Sorry?" She didn't know what else to say. Maybe, *touch me before I die from need*?

He nipped her earlobe, the little flash of pain bringing her up on her toes.

"Now it's your turn."

She made the mistake of tilting her head back to look at him. The no-nonsense expression on his face spiked her temperature. His deep command brought it to boiling point. "Up against the wall."

Abby's legs quivered like gelatin. Lucky for her, he took charge, kicking the door shut and guiding her to the opposite wall. A nudge of his hips urged her closer. When she was flat against the surface he removed his hands from her wrists and ran them slowly down the inside of her arms.

She trembled beneath the gentle assault. When he squeezed her sides, she pressed her forehead against the hard surface in front of her and gulped for air.

"Nothing so far," he growled.

Her insides clenched. She went up on her toes even as she leaned further into his hard body.

His fingers followed the indentation of her waistline and gently scooped the curves before splaying out across her hips. "Hmmm."

Abby bit her lip and rolled her cheek against the wall. The hard bulge at her lower back said he was just as turned on by this power play.

"I think this needs more investigation."

Yes. Please.

She didn't say the words aloud, but she might as well have. No longer in control of her body, she undulated against him, a clear signal for more.

His left hand slid beneath her shirt and palmed the soft skin of her lower belly, holding her still while he simultaneously thrust against her.

A keening cry of need escaped her. She rolled her head against his shoulder. Tugging her hair with his right hand, he angled her face to the side then finally, finally! claimed her lips.

Fireworks exploded through her bloodstream.

Abby needed to touch him, any part of him, but her arms were trapped between her body and the wall. She curled her fingers against the surface, scratching mindlessly while a moan bubbled inside her.

Glen deepened their kiss. Their tongues dueled, slid against one another, mimicking the movements of their bodies. He bent his knees and thrust against her, withdrew and thrust again. She ground her bottom into the cradle of his hips and oh, God, he *rubbed* her in response.

Breathing hurt, but she didn't complain. Not for anything in the world would she stop this. She needed him, and his kiss, like a drug. One that raced through her bloodstream and pushed her to a high that was so close, perspiration beaded on her forehead and her legs started to shake.

If only he would...

With his right hand, he tweaked her nipple.

Her head slammed into his chest. Everything inside her seized up, then fractured.

"There you go." His rough whisper was reassuring, but when he lowered his hand and pressed the heel of his palm between her thighs, she seized trembled and broke into a million tiny pieces.

He drew every last pulse of orgasm from her body until she collapsed, limp, against the wall.

Too heavy to keep open, she let her eyes slide closed and rested her cheek on the smooth surface.

His fingers slid beneath her shirt hem and gently stroked her belly. He nuzzled her earlobe and sipped at the tender place where her neck and shoulder met.

She wanted to say something. *Thank you*? But she was too exhausted for words.

Long moments passed. The strength in her legs returned. The bulge pressing into the small of her back remained hard, waiting for her to recuperate. When she made a small move with her hands and lifted her face, he stepped away, only to scoop her into his arms. Blue gaze alive with desire, he rumbled, "Your room?"

Speaking was still impossible, so she simply pointed around the short wall facing the entry and past the living room fireplace to a door on the other side.

Her bed was made, for a change, though one side was covered with stacks of paper, notebooks, two or three pens, and a calculator.

He grinned on seeing it.

"Don't tell my brothers," she muttered.

"Never." He gave her a quick kiss and set her down on her feet.

She cleared everything from the comforter. The moment she dropped the last stack in the corner, he was there again, wrapping his arms around her and devouring her mouth with his as he walked her backward to the bed. Her knees hit the side of the mattress, and she fell back onto the comforter.

He followed her down without breaking the kiss, twisting at the last minute so his weight fell to the side.

It was Abby's turn to touch. Like a beggar too long denied a feast, she tugged the hem of his shirt up over his lean torso, breaking the kiss so he could pull it over his head. Taking full advantage of his momentary blindness, she kissed his abs, licked his chest, swirled her tongue around the flat disc of one nipple. His body jerked, tensed, and she did it again.

"Oh, baby."

She liked that sound. Wanting to hear more, she kissed the nipple and ran her left hand down his front to stroke the length of his erection through his jeans.

He jackknifed against the comforter. She flipped over and straddled his thighs with her hips, stroking him with her hand and making love to him with her mouth.

"Do you like this?" She slid her fingers through his dark hair and lightly scraped his scalp. He dug his heels into the mattress and thrust up, almost dislodging her. "I take that as a yes."

Now it was his turn to pant.

She rubbed her breasts against his torso and squeezed his thighs between her own.

"You have too many clothes on," he complained, reaching for the bottom of her shirt.

"Let me."

Abby enjoyed this. Making sure she had his full attention, she slowly pulled the hem of her shirt up. One inch and her lower abdomen was revealed. Two inches and her navel appeared. He took a deep breath, eyes blazing. Another inch and the bottom of her bra was exposed. Not a sexy garment, but a full-figure support article. She referred to it as a Sherman tank, but he seemed to like it if the way he ran his hands over the band and up over the cups was any indication.

"Show me more."

Just like that the power shifted again. When she lifted her arms to remove the shirt, he stayed her hands, so it remained over her eyes.

"Stop."

The whispered command brooked no argument and he wasn't going to get one from her. Not when he gently scraped the inside of her arms with his fingernails. Not when he reached behind her and released the clasp of her bra then pushed the cups up over her breasts, freeing them to the cool air. She felt her nipples pucker from the cold. They hurt, but he took care of them. Cupping one with a warm palm, he tongued the other. Oh, God, he *licked* it. The slow stroke of his tongue made her whole body sway, silently begging him to do it again.

"Take off your shirt."

She threw it to the floor.

"The bra."

It went into the farthest corner.

He circled each breast with his thumb and forefinger. He lifted them and laved her nipples with his tongue while she rocked back and forth on his thighs.

Advance. Retreat. Seek. Escape when the sensations were too much for her to bear, only to have him pursue.

He showed no mercy.

When he finally took one nipple into the warm cavern of his mouth and looked directly at her, eyes blazing, she convulsed with a mini orgasm. Her eyes slid shut and her head fell back, rolling from side to side as the sweet torment of her breasts continued.

"Like this?" he asked, as if there were any question.

Her voice sounded like she had marbles in her mouth. "You're a master at this."

"I'm going to master you."

Yes! For fifteen years she had been waiting for someone, not just anyone but this man, to take that responsibility.

"Abby?"

"Yes. Please."

"Open your eyes."

Pulling herself from the sensual fog surrounding her, she blinked. Once. Twice. Focused on his handsome features. At the trim beard gently abrading her breast while his tongue flicked over her nipple.

"I'm going to stop now."

Her eyes flew open wide. "No!"

His smile warmed every part of her. "We have too many clothes on."

She was probably grinning like a fool, but the man was so exciting! And hot. Definitely hot. Something on full display when he rolled away from her and came to his feet. His wide shoulders and long, lean torso narrowed down to trim hips cradling an impressive bulge. For her.

Flicking the button open on his jeans, he slid the zipper down while she watched with anticipation. He slipped his fingers beneath the metal teeth and fisted his erection with one hand. She was jealous of that hand.

"Now you."

Abby liked this game. Enthusiastically she put her thumbs inside the waistband of her yoga pants and rolled the material down an inch. Two. And stopped. "You're next."

His grin was a white slash of teeth, his eyes a sizzling blue. "Anything for the lady."

The jeans only made it to his upper thighs before a discordant noise shattered the steamy privacy of her bedroom.

"Shit." He yanked his pants up and slid a cell phone from the back pocket.

Abby scooted across the comforter and leaned against the headboard, wrapping her arms around her knees. She felt exposed, as if the person on the other end of the line could see what they were doing, could invade their privacy just as the call had.

Glen ran his fingers through his hair and turned away from her. This couldn't be good.

"Shit."

No. No, no, no! He would only say that a second time if the call meant he had to leave.

The expression on his face when he turned back to her confirmed it even before he spoke. "My daughter is sick again."

Chapter Six

Glen couldn't leave Abby's condo in his present condition, or the kids would have a million questions for him. He tugged his shirt on, retrieved her clothes for her, then paced the length of the bedroom to exorcise his frustration and bring his body under control.

"She's been sick on and off for a few weeks," he explained, wanting her to know he wouldn't leave if he could avoid it. "Doctors are running some tests, but they haven't come up with anything yet."

"It's okay," she mumbled through the shirt she was pulling on.

"No. It's not." This was important to him. When she stood next to the bed, withdrawing in every sense of the word, he closed the distance between them and took her shoulders in his hands, forcing her to look at him. "It's not."

"What other choice do you have?"

"None. But this, you and me, isn't over. Not by a long shot."

She lifted one shoulder in a shrug to indicate it was no big deal. A lie and they both knew it.

"Spend the night with me." The impulsive offer came out of nowhere, but as soon as the words left his mouth, they felt right. "With us."

She tilted her head back and met his gaze, her gray-green eyes wide and her chestnut hair rolling across her shoulder. Resisting the urge to bury his face in that thick mane, he pulled her closer and said, "Jason and Sara are having a snowmobiling party tonight. Come with me. Meet the kids."

"Okay," she breathed against his shirtfront.

He wanted to stay for the day. The night. Several nights. Instead, he eased away from her and walked to the front door.

Like a hostess seeing her guest out, she trailed along behind him, but he didn't face her until his outerwear was on.

She looked a little sad, a little dazed, and a whole lot of tempting. Glen palmed her flushed cheeks and kissed her one more time. Hard.

"If Darcy is feeling better, what do you say to a sleepover?"

Confusion pleated the smooth skin of her brow. "I'm not sure what you mean."

"I'll see the kids safely into bed, and then we'll have a grown-up pajama party. You. Me. Here."

A slow smile dawned across her pretty features.

"Without the pajamas."

****

At six o'clock he and the kids stood waiting outside her door. They had been harassing him ever since he said he had a date, trying to guess who it might be, trying to bribe him into giving them more details. He finally told them it was the woman across the hall, which only encouraged them.

"That doesn't tell us anything," Darcy complained, in full health again after an afternoon of soup and rest.

"I'll bet it's the lady from the wedding," Colin guessed.

"Well, you're a big help. Want to narrow it down for me?"

"You know, the one at his table that he wasn't looking at when we asked to go for the champagne."

"Don't be stupid. If he wasn't looking at her, how could she be the one?"

"You really don't know anything about men, do you?" Which was a good thing as far as Glen was concerned.

"Fine. Then I'll bet you twenty dollars you don't know what you're talking about."

Colin's smile was smug. "Short like a twelve-year-old." He held his hand up to indicate a height equal to his breastbone. "Thick, reddish-brown hair." His fingers made fluffing motions around his head and down to his shoulders. "And a body like this." When he cupped his hands then drew them closer together, indicating ample breasts and a smaller waistline, Glen almost choked. Since when had this kid become so damned observant?

Their conversation came to an abrupt halt when Abby opened the door. Her eyes sparkled with anticipation, and her cheeks were as pink as the piping on her black down coat. He wanted to take her in his arms right there in front of the kids.

Instead, he introduced her. "Abby, this is my son Colin and my daughter Darcy." They exchanged greetings. "Ready to go?"

"I'll get the elevator." Darcy hurried to the call button. While they waited for the car, she looked Abby over, and he could see her impression was favorable even before she said, "You're really pretty."

"Thank you."

"And I like your doorbell. The music it plays."

A ping preceded the elevator car reaching their floor. When the doors opened with a swish, Glen put a hand to the small of Abby's back and ushered her inside, mostly because he wanted an excuse to touch her. His daughter watched the movement closely. Colin, on the other hand, was playing Mr. Cool and held the doors open while purposefully not looking at either of them.

"I think I saw you at the wedding," he said, oh so nonchalantly, when they were all inside. "You were at Dad's table, weren't you?"

"That's right," Abby confirmed, surprise in her voice.

"I remember faces." He hit the button to start their descent. "Especially on pretty women."

Glen raised his eyebrows at Colin, who pretended not to see it. Leaning close to his sister, he stage whispered, "You owe me twenty bucks."

****

Jason and Sara's house was on the northeast side of town, just off the road to the quarry he managed. Glen's kids filled the few minutes' drive there with questions for Abby.

"Have you always lived here?" Darcy asked.

"No," she answered. "I've lived in lots of places."

"Like where?"

"Well, we were in New York when I was little. Then my parents split up and Mom got a job teaching at UVM, so I went back and forth between the city and Burlington for a while."

"Did you like that?"

"I loved both places, but I hated the travel. And the uncertainty."

"What do you mean?"

Glen was curious about her explanation, too.

"I mean, there was always a pull between the two houses. Two sets of everything. Two beds, two pets, two bikes, two sets of friends. Everything. I just wanted to be in one place that was all mine."

"Like us."

Before Abby could comment, Colin joined in. "Where else did you live?"

"Well, when Dad had made a name for himself, he only needed to have a gallery in New York, not work there, so he moved to Manchester, Vermont, with his girlfriend."

"Are they still there?"

"He is, but his girlfriend Flo left after my little brother was out of high school. She's in New York again."

"So basically, your whole family is in Vermont."

"I guess so. I never really thought about it before, but I guess we're all Vermonters. My immediate family, anyway."

"But the rest live somewhere else?"

"My grandparents on my father's side live on Andros Island. That's in the Bahamas. My other grandparents live in Yazoo County,

Mississippi. I used to spend my summers between their houses, and I still go to see them all at least once a year."

"Cool," Colin said.

Darcy, like the most dogged investigative reporter, wasn't done yet. "You said you have a little brother. Is he the only one, or do you have brothers and sisters?"

"Three brothers. The oldest one, David, bought The Gables a few weeks ago."

"I thought Aunt Linda said a Chinaman bought it."

"He *is* Chinese."

"How does that work?"

"What do you say we give Abby a break and stop with the third degree?" Glen interrupted. "Besides, we're here."

***

The sweeping arc of the car's headlights revealed a cape-style home below the main road. Nestled among towering, nude maple trees and backed by evergreens cloaked in winter's protective white raiment, it could feature on a postcard for the Northeast Kingdom.

Snowmobiles lined the banks of Somerset River a hundred yards behind the house.

Little white lights danced between the trees lining the dead-end road that doubled as the driveway. At the end of that stretch, an abandoned cottage watched through sightless windows while they parked by the shed across from the house.

"What a wonderful location." Abby had handled the real estate transaction for Sara when she bought the property a year ago, but she had never seen the place.

"Jason's sister used to live here when we were younger," Glen said, "when his son Andrew was little." He turned off the ignition and the four of them got out of the car. He offered her his elbow, and she wrapped her mittened hand around his sleeve. "We spent a lot of time in these woods. It was kind of a homecoming for him, moving in after the wedding."

"When are you going to buy that place for us, Dad?" Colin asked, leading the way to the picket fence marking the cape's front yard, but nodding toward the cottage.

"I don't know." Glen's long-suffering tone implied he fielded the question on a regular basis.

"Jason said the owner is ready to sell."

"We'll see." Glen unlatched the gate and stood back for the kids to precede them down the path to the front door.

"It would be so cool, even if it was only on weekends." Darcy turned around, walking backwards while adding, "This is our favorite place on the planet, Abby. You're so lucky to live here full time."

"I think so."

"You're staying?" This seemingly offhand question came from Colin, though Abby suspected there was more to it, given the sudden tension in Glen's arm.

"I have no plans to leave." Somerset was her home by choice, not by birth or by accident. With David buying The Gables, she hoped it would be home to both of them for a long time. She imagined the two of them having families, their children growing up together, sharing holidays.

"And we're here," Glen announced.

Inside, the house was all warmth and light, from the kitchen full of guests on their right to the corner fireplace in the dining room on the left where a golden retriever lay on the braided hearth rug. Seeing them, the dog raised its head, eyes hopeful and tail wagging. Both teenagers knelt to pet it.

"Can I take your coat?" Glen asked.

"Yes, please." She unzipped it and turned her back so he could help her out of it.

She had been desperate to continue what they started this morning but equally desperate not to think about it. Yet when his hands lingered on her shoulders longer than necessary before sliding the garment free, she closed her eyes and took a slow, deep breath. He was so close she could smell his light cologne. He put her coat on a peg beside the door and hung his own coat on top of it. A quiver ran through her belly as she imagined him wrapping his body around hers.

"Sorry about the inquisition in the car," he said.

"I'm a lawyer. I can take it."

They shared a smile, and he slid his arm around her waist. "Maybe—

His reply was interrupted when Jason emerged from the kitchen.

"Abby!" His eyes slid to Glen's possessive hold, but he said only, "It's good to see you again."

Sara joined them, butting Jason with her elbow until he opened his arms and she slipped into his hold.

The gesture spoke to a couple being familiar with one another's body language, a silent communication Abby longed to have with a partner. Not just anyone, either, but the man at her side.

"Where are the kids?" Sara asked.

Glen pointed his thumb in the direction of the dining room.

"Ah. Spoiling Cortland." On hearing his name, the golden retriever thumped its tail.

"Hope you like fish, Abby. Glen and Jason make a fishing trip to the Finger Lakes every year, and we're cooking up some of last summer's catch."

"I never met a fish I didn't love. To eat, that is."

"Good." Jason kissed the top of Sara's head. "You can have my wife's share too."

At his words, a blush suffused Sara's heart-shaped face while his countenance fairly glowed with pride. What was this?

Glen didn't seem to know any more than she did. "Are you on a no-fish diet or something?" he asked.

"Nothing she can't recover from in, say, about nine months, give or take the last eight weeks."

Abby understood the term pregnant pause, because for just a moment, no one moved or said anything. Then Glen slid his arm from her waist and punched Jason on the shoulder. "Congratulations, man."

"Thanks. We're pretty happy about it."

Stealing Sara from his hold, Glen lifted her until her feet dangled several inches above the floor. "Sweetheart, I can't thank you enough for making this guy smile every day."

"I love him." That simple. That profound.

"And I love you for it."

They hugged briefly, then he returned her to Jason, who welcomed her as if she had been gone for hours instead of a minute or two.

A pang of longing hit Abby, mixed with hope and excitement that she might be on her way to having something like they did.

"In case you haven't figured it out," Sara said to her, "we'll be having our first child sometime next July. I haven't had an ultrasound yet, so the date isn't exact."

"Congratulations to both of you."

Darcy barreled past them and threw her arms around Jason. "Oh my God, I can't believe it! Can I babysit? Please?" Without giving him a chance to answer, she turned to Sara. "I promise I'll take excellent care of him. Or her. I don't care what it is. Do you care?"

Sara laughed at her exuberance. "Healthy is good. Although I think my husband may have a preference."

"I'll never get tired of hearing those words." Still holding onto the teenager, he kissed his wife on the lips. "*My husband*. Music to my ears."

"Are you two always this mushy?" Colin demanded, joining them from the dining room. "Or do people lose all sense of decorum when they get married and automatically make fools of themselves in public?"

"Big word," Jason mocked. "Come closer and I'll show you some decorum."

The threat was obviously an empty one, because he reached out with one arm, pulled the teen close, and thumped him on the back.

"Saaara, the fish is gonna burn if you don't get your butt in here and start playing hostess again," Jimmy Duncan called from the kitchen. He waved a spatula above the heads of several guests and sent her a panicked look.

"Be right there, buddy."

Their hosts went back to the stove, and Glen introduced Abby to the other guests. Seventeen people crowded into the kitchen and dining room, laughing and eating until the windows fogged up and Cortland retreated to another room for some peace and quiet.

When the plates were finally empty and the dishwasher loaded, they tumbled out the back door into the clear winter night. Glen led Abby down the line of snowmobiles to where Colin was already straddling one machine and Darcy prepared to mount the one beside it.

"Uh-uh," Glen said. "This time you'll be riding with your brother."

"But I always—oh," she finished, eyes wide with comprehension, moving back and waving toward the abandoned seat. "Here you go, Abby."

Abby didn't bother to object because after watching him for the past hour and having to share him with everyone else, she couldn't wait to get close to him again.

He swung his long legs over the seat and slid forward to make room for her. When she climbed on behind him, her thighs lay against his. He patted her left calf and told her to move closer. When no space separated them, he took her hands and wrapped them around his middle.

"Hold on!"

She squeezed once to let him know she heard, then they were off, screaming along the riverbank at full throttle. They plunged through the trees at the back of the property, snaked through the forest, rose and fell with the terrain. If he threw his body to the left, she followed; to the right, she went right.

Suddenly they sailed into the air and emerged from into an open field. Abby shouted with joy.

They sped across the moonlit landscape, so bright it looked like midday. The engine purred. Diesel fumes evaporated into the cold, still air. Her eyes watered. She pressed her cheek against his hard back and savored every minute of it.

At the edge of the field, they dove into the woods again, coming out high above the quarry. In every direction dark mountains slumbered beneath the pearlescent sky.

"Like it?" Glen turned his head to ask the question, and she answered with a kiss. Long, full of tongue, exuberant, and reciprocated. She couldn't tell if the growl she heard was coming from the sled they were on or the man, but she didn't care. Both excited her.

The kids pulled up beside them.

"You two should get a room," Colin smirked.

"We just might," Glen fired back.

Darcy groaned. "Can we puh-leeze not talk about this?"

Laughing, Glen revved the engine before taking off across the ridge with the kids following close behind them. Soon they caught up with Jimmy and Glen's sister Linda. Eventually the whole group assembled in a field on the other side of the quarry where acres of open land stretched out along the river, separated into neat squares by posts and fence line.

"I'll go ahead," Peter Tremblay said. Abby recognized him as the young potter who sold his wares on the common at last year's Independence Day parade. "It's my folks' land so I know where the gates are," he explained. "Someone needs to bring up the rear and shut them behind us, though."

"We'll do it," Glen volunteered.

The pastures were not as exciting as the twisting trail through the woods, but Abby loved flying full throttle across the wintry landscape with the moon darting just ahead of them across the mirror-like surface.

She held on tight to Glen.

She felt his every move despite their winter gear. Could he feel it when she rubbed her body against his back?

The throb of the engine heightened her need for him. The crisp night air cooled her feverish cheeks, but only he could quell the fire raging inside her.

At the end of the last paddock, they turned north and rode along an abandoned railroad bed in the lowlands beside the river. It was bumpier than the field. Each hill they topped sent a jolt through her body and increased the tension between them.

She couldn't be the only one feeling it, could she?

By the time they crossed the road at the bridge and pulled into Jason and Sara's yard, her legs trembled around his hard thighs. He turned off the snowmobile and she slid back on the seat, desperate to gain some control.

The last engine rattled into silence. "Anyone for hot chocolate?" Sara asked.

Most of the party accepted her offer.

Abby wasn't sure she could walk, so she waited for Glen to agree, but without a word he got off the machine and pulled Jason aside.

She didn't move while they talked. She didn't dare.

Jason clapped Glen on the back and turned toward the house while Glen returned to where she waited.

She lifted one foot to disembark, but he scooped her off the back of the sled and down the length of his body until she stood on the ground, trembling all over again.

"That's for torturing me through those fields," he murmured.

She laughed because it was either that or cry. "I didn't think you noticed."

"I did. And now we're going home to finish what you started."

As desperate as she was to take him up on that offer, they hadn't come alone. "What about the kids?"

"They're spending the night with Jason and Sara."

Chapter Seven

Glen was too old to pretend when it came to what he wanted. As soon as the elevator doors slid shut behind them, he nudged Abby back against the wall and lifted her off the floor for a kiss. She wrapped one leg around his hip and rubbed her core against the hard bulge he had been sporting ever since she climbed onto the snowmobile behind him.

Scraping her nails across his scalp now, she broke the kiss and whispered, "Don't hold back."

Her honest response turned his smoldering desire into an all-out flame. He recaptured her mouth in a hard kiss. She stretched to get closer and he hoisted her up until she locked her ankles at the base of his spine. He speared his hands into her thick hair while their tongues dueled, and their bodies rocked against each other.

The ping of the elevator barely registered before the doors opened to the third floor. Crossing the lobby without breaking their embrace, he pulled his mouth from hers just long enough to say, "Put in the code."

Abby blindly swatted at the wall. After a few misses, she got the security code entered, and they stumbled backward into her condo unit. He yanked her boots off one at a time, dropping them to the floor before kicking off his own. Her hat and mittens were tossed over his shoulder. She tugged at the zipper of his coat.

They left a trail of scattered outerwear from the front door to her bedroom, but he couldn't care less. She was his tonight. No kids, no work, no misunderstandings between them. Just two desperate, consenting adults.

By the time they fell onto her comforter, they were struggling to breathe. Her button-front sweater was open and dangling from the elbows, his shirt was pushed up to the top of his chest, the snap on his jeans undone.

"I've dreamed of this," she gasped, disengaging her arms so she could throw off her sweater and unsnap her bra while he stood and shucked off the rest of his clothing.

"I haven't dreamed of anything else," he admitted, amazed he could think at all with her glorious body unveiled. "Come here."

She walked on her knees across the comforter to the end of the bed, breasts swaying, abdomen rippling, and he almost came from watching her.

She stopped inches away from him, her lush mouth curved into a teasing smile. "Is this close enough?"

"Not hardly." Tugging on her belt loops with his fingers, he drew her forward until their torsos met, and the feel of her soft skin against his sent a shudder through his body. He unsnapped her pants and slid his hands inside, palming her buttocks. They were cold from the snowmobile run, yet soft and supple.

"Perfect," he growled. "But still not close enough."

She held her hand up to ward him off, wriggled out of her remaining clothes and tossed them onto the floor before coming up onto her knees again.

He knew a lot of women shaved or waxed below the waist, but it surprised him that she was bare, and he was a little disappointed. He had imagined dark curls adorning that special place.

"It's for swimming," she whispered, as if she had read his thoughts. "It's more comfortable in a tight suit, and it reduces the drag."

"Ah." Of course. Although she obviously cared about her appearance, this was a practical reason he could appreciate.

Cupping her shoulders, he slid his hands over her breasts, and belly, stopping at her hips. "I told you I would go down on my knees for you."

Confusion crossed her face, quickly followed by surprise when he dropped to the floor. Her belly quivered and her legs trembled. He slid his fingers up the back of her thighs and squeezed. She was soft and golden everywhere. Curvy but strong.

He kissed her inner thigh. She jerked in his hold.

He nuzzled the spot with his nose, and she fisted her hands in his hair.

"Touch me," she groaned.

He glanced up to find her gray-green eyes glazed with need. No way could he ignore the plea in them.

Parting the folds of her sex with his thumbs, he blew a warm puff of air against the small kernel of flesh between them and watched as her skin flushed and her eyes dimmed.

He blew again and she folded over at the waist, a hiss escaping her lips.

"So sensitive," he marveled.

"Touch me!" A demand this time, accompanied by a thrust of her hips.

Glen pushed down on her clit with one thumb. She threw her head back and bit her lip, long hair flowing down her spine.

Replacing his thumb with his mouth, he kissed her. A high whine escaped her mouth and she almost buckled over before jerking upright again.

He suckled that small kernel of flesh.

Abby's eyes flew open, staring at him as he made love to her with his mouth.

He slid one hand up her soft belly and palmed her breast. When she pushed into that hold, he gently twisted her nipple. She gasped. He increased the pressure, with his mouth, with his fingers, and her hands flailed uselessly in the air before landing on his shoulders.

"Better hold on tight," he murmured against her, then slid one finger home to test her readiness.

"Oh, my God."

If his mouth was free, he would second that thought. He'd never known a woman this responsive. To have her lush body under his command, to watch her flush with pleasure and undulate above him, was an unparalleled high. He didn't know how long he could please her, though, before losing control. She made him feel like an adolescent all over again. Like the first time. No, better than the first time because now he knew what he was doing.

He slid a second finger into her warm, wet sheath, and she exploded around him. One moment the muscles of her thighs and abdomen went rigid, the next she was shaking like a leaf in a gale force wind. He grasped her nipple, hard, at the same time he sucked her into his mouth. A broken cry fell from her lips, and her head rolled from shoulder to shoulder.

When the last contraction passed and she went limp in his hold, perspiration coating her golden breasts, abdomen, and thighs. He wanted to lick every drop from her flesh.

"Abby?"

"Hmmm?"

Her eyes were closed. She didn't seem to hear him.

Slowly Glen withdrew his mouth. He slid his hand from her breast and ran his thumb over her clit. Softly, but still a ripple of aftershock went through her. He moved that hand to her hip and gently withdrew the other one from her body, resting it on her thigh.

Blinking, she looked down at him through eyes glazed with passion. She looked ready for a long, warm nap while he was still painfully hard.

Careful not to startle her with any quick movements, he reached over with one hand and slid a condom from the back pocket of his jeans where they lay on the floor. Thank God he had thought ahead to put one there. He had more in his coat, but he didn't want to break contact with her to go and get one.

He tore the packet open with his teeth. When she leaned forward and watched with curiosity, he smiled and slid the condom on.

"I'm on the pill," she told him.

He believed her but he had heard that before. Plus, there were the other considerations.

As if reading his mind, she said, "I haven't had a lover in two years." His surprise must have shown on his face. "Look where I live. I'm a lawyer and a judge. I can't indiscriminately sleep with people and keep my reputation as a professional, and it's not like there are bars or dance clubs around here to go to on a Friday night."

He didn't want her in a bar or a nightclub. *Whoa*, that reaction shocked him so much he stood abruptly only to watch as she tumbled back onto the comforter.

"Glen?"

Still wondering where this sudden possessiveness came from, because he had never experienced it before, he came down on the bed beside her.

Tamping down those dark emotions, he said, "It's been eighteen months for me. Clean bill of health, but you can never be too careful."

"Then what are you waiting for?"

Laughing, he rolled over and slid between her welcoming thighs. She placed her hands on his shoulders, he put his forearms on either side of her body to keep from crushing her.

Perspiration trickled down the slopes of her ample breasts to rosy, pink nipples. He loved the contrast between their color and her golden skin. Ducking his head, he laved them with his tongue, once, twice, stopping when she moved restlessly beneath him.

"Don't tease me." Her voice was husky with need. "I need you. Please, Glen."

Hearing his name on her sweet lips was more than he could handle, and he slid home.

"Yesss." She arched her back, and he wanted to kiss her exposed neck, but short of being a contortionist, there was no way he could bend to reach her.

Resting his weight on one forearm, he used his other hand to palm her buttocks. She wrapped her legs around him, her thighs clenching his lower back while her inner muscles contracted around him.

She stroked his back with small, agile hands. They scraped across his chest and delved between their bodies.

He had never had a lover touch him like that during sex. Abby cupped the base of his erection so every time he moved the friction between them heightened. When she stroked herself, he almost lost his breath. With her other hand she squeezed his buttocks and scored the backs of his thighs with her nails.

He convulsed above her.

"I dreamed about this."

She talks. Could the woman possibly turn him on any more than he already was?

She thrust her pelvis up to meet his, whispering, "I dreamed about this. With you."

Glen lost it.

With little finesse and no attempt at rhythm, he thrust into her welcoming body. Once. Twice. Then he threw his head back, leg muscles rigid, exploding inside her.

His heartbeat went from a gallop to a canter to a slow trot. He pulled in great gulps of air and brought his forearms, weak and trembling in the aftermath, to rest on either side of her head.

Her breath came in soft pants against his chest, and he closed his eyes to enjoy the feeling. He was sure there must be nothing left inside of him to give.

Until she raised her head and gently bit his nipple, proving he wasn't done after all.

****

Abby took a sip of red wine and set her glass on the nightstand, snuggling closer to his hard, warm chest. The bedding protected her modesty but rode low on his torso.

"And such a beautiful torso it is," she murmured.

Glen stilled against her cheek. "What was that?"

"I said, you've got a great body."

He relaxed again and she played with the dark whorls of hair running between his pecs down toward his navel.

His gaze was on the large painting suspended from the ceiling over her bed. Modern and abstract, a brilliant splash of orange and reds and blues in her father's signature style.

"You told the kids you summered with your grandparents?" he asked somewhat absently.

Taking advantage of his distractedness, she slid one hand beneath the covers and lightly stroked his thigh while she talked. "I spent most summers with my grandparents. At least two months each year as an out-islander. Pa was a fisherman, and I was his first mate. Ma ran a fruit stand. She knows all the locals, and she introduced me to them each summer as if it was the first time I'd been there. She said that way they would remember me when I grew up and came back again. Not mistake me for an American."

He swirled the wine in his glass, seeming lost in the reflection from her bedside lamps on the burgundy liquid. "You're not a US citizen?"

"I am now, but children of a Bahamian father take his citizenship, so I didn't choose to be American until I was ready for the bar exam. Anyway, in the Bahamas you're referred to by your original nationality even if you have citizenship, so there were always people asking where I was from. Ma wanted them to see me as a local because Americans can be resented there. A tourist thing."

"Hmm."

Abby loved the way his chest vibrated when he spoke. It was like the purring of a cat, only magnified by his size so it hummed through her whole body and made her want to stretch against him.

"What about your other grandparents?"

"I'd spend at least two weeks with them after coming back from the Bahamas. Grampa Kelly was a long-haul trucker for UPS, but he always took time off in the middle of August to see me. Grammie Kelly stayed home and took care of the house and garden, the family."

"But your parents didn't follow in their footsteps?"

Sighing because she finally had the man in her bed after fifteen years of pining for him, and he wanted to go over her family tree, she removed her hand from beneath the covers and reached for her glass of wine. Taking a sip and settling back against the pillows, she answered, "Not a chance. Dad couldn't wait to move to the States and live in the city. He goes home to visit, but Mom's a different story. When she left the Delta, she never looked back."

He refilled his now empty glass and when she nodded in response to his silent inquiry, topped hers off as well.

"I grew up on a dairy farm," he volunteered.

"The one across from your sister's diner?"

He nodded. "My grandparents owned it, and we lived with them when I was young. My Quebec grandparents would come down and help during busy seasons, calving and haying and maple syrup. My American grandparents passed away, so now Mom and Dad are the older generation, and my brother Roger runs it. He's training Bryce to take over from him someday."

"But you wanted to live in the city?"

Body suddenly tensing against hers, he shook his head. "No. I wanted to live here. My divorce killed those plans."

"Why?"

"C'mon, Abby, you were in the courtroom that day. My ex-wife shredded my reputation. I was a bank manager. That meant you had to live a conservative lifestyle, especially in the country, so people would trust you with their money. No way could I recover from the rumors spreading after that day."

"But what she said about you..." Abby faltered. "It was, I mean, it wasn't like you were abusive, or a lecher or something."

"You can't even get the words out," he teased, relaxing again. "She said I was a sex fiend and couldn't live without it. That wouldn't have been so bad, but she also said I was into BDSM, which no one talked about back then. Of course, that was an exaggeration. Typical for her."

"You mean you're *not* into BDSM?"

"Do I like the idea of seeing a woman tied, whipped, clamped, and plugged?" He seemed to ponder the idea before rolling onto his side and facing her. "Nope." His smile proved he hadn't considered the lifestyle for even a minute. "Just good, old-fashioned sex." He shrugged. "With maybe an occasional tying just to spice things up." He grinned. "Sorry to disappoint you."

"Disappointment? If what just happened is disappointment, then go ahead and break my heart. My only complaint is that you seem content with just one round."

Blue eyes gleaming, he took the wineglass from her hand and set it on the nightstand. The movement brought his chest into contact with hers, and she barely resisted the urge to rub against him.

"You enjoyed playing with me a few minutes ago, didn't you?" He dipped a finger into his wineglass, then dropped a red pearl of liquid onto the slope of her breast. "Thought I wasn't paying attention or that maybe I wasn't interested?"

The wine trickled a slow path over her skin.

He followed it with his tongue.

Abby's thighs clenched and her toes curled. When he set his drink aside and slid the comforter down to her waist, the breath stuttered in her chest.

He cupped one breast in his hand and circled her nipple with his thumb. "I left marks on you."

She didn't understand.

"With my beard. Here"—he stroked the side of her breast—"and on your thighs."

"It's okay." *Just don't stop.*

"No, it's not." With a wicked smile he curled his tongue around one hard nipple. Warm and wet and so good she dug her heels into the mattress. "Let me kiss it and make it better."

****

While Abby slept, Glen slipped across the hall to his condo for a cup of coffee. He had a quick shower, threw on a clean pair of jeans, and returned to find her still out. She didn't stir when he slid onto the comforter beside her, so he took a sip of coffee and resumed his study of the painting above them.

By the time his cup was empty, Abby started to wake. Her face scrunched up like a little kid hit with daylight. She rolled onto her side and curled into a ball. Moments later she groaned and flopped onto her back. She flung her arm out and when it landed against his bare chest with a loud slap, her eyes flew open. She jackknifed up off the mattress.

"Good morning," he grinned.

Abby blinked, once, twice, then settled back into the covers with a soft, "Good morning to you."

Glen lifted an arm in invitation, and she curled against his side. He put his empty cup down and looked again at the bright ceiling art.

"My father's work," she explained.

"It's powerful."

"Hmmm. You might leave the Bahamas, but they never leave you."

"Is that a saying there?"

"No. Just mine."

She twisted and grabbed a photo from the nightstand, holding it out for him to see. "Law school graduation day."

A tall, spare man with caramel skin and a mop of dark curls stood in the center with one arm around Abby, the other around a round, dark woman he recognized from the living room portrait. Abby was dressed in a black cap and gown, her grandmother in a bright floral dress and matching turban.

"Did you always want to be a lawyer?"

"No. I always liked logic, though, and of course I loved language. Latin helps a lot."

He studied the photo for a long moment. She bore no resemblance to her father, but her proud smile matched the one on her grandmother's face. Both women beamed for the camera.

"What about your mom?"

Putting that picture back, she took another from the nightstand. This one of a woman on a sidewalk with a wild mane of red hair holding a picket sign. Her expression was as severe as the dark clothing she wore.

Abby grimaced. "She's not exactly the life of the party."

"I'm not going to touch that statement."

"Mom cares about me, but she is always on a mission. Always fighting for some cause. I was lucky to have my grandmothers and David's mother, Flo."

Glen rolled onto his side, silently encouraging her to continue.

"When I was little, Mom liked men as long as they were starving artists, social dissidents, or unappreciated writers."

"She doesn't like men?"

"Hates them. The more successful they are, the more she holds them responsible for all the world's evils."

Glen wasn't in a hurry to meet her.

Abby replaced that photo and held up another. "You know two of my brothers." David stood behind her in the shot, his chin resting on top of her head, Romney towering above them with two fingers held up, bunny-ear style. All three of them were grinning. In the background a cerulean sky met an endless expanse of blue-green sea.

"I love this picture."

"Where is it?"

"At my grandparents' house."

"Tell me about it."

"Every time I look at this, I can almost smell the sea breeze and hear the way it sounds when it ripples through the palm trees. The hot air tastes like fresh fruit and rum."

It seemed his logical little judge was something of an artist herself, but a poet instead of a painter. Wait, *his* judge?

Before he could dwell on that thought, she took the final photo from the nightstand.

"This is Hume, ten years ago."

A skinny boy with curly, red-brown hair and a freckled face stuck his tongue out for the photographer while poking a finger in each ear.

"He's not fond of having his picture taken," Abby explained.

"Your mother's son?" At her nod, he clarified, "But she hates men?"

"I know." Abby grimaced. "One of life's more ironic twists. Artificial insemination and she got a boy."

She put the photo away and turned back to snuggle against him. "Enough about family," she murmured, sliding her hand across his middle and counting his ribs with her fingers. "I can think of much better things to do with this hot body."

The comment caught him off guard, but he told himself not to read anything into it. So, she was done talking. After his ex-wife bagged him like a pretty prize only to discard him later, he was sensitive to women wanting him only for what was on the outside.

He couldn't let his own insecurities get in the way of their relationship.

Clearing the emotional baggage from his throat, he said, "What time do you swim today?"

"Usually at eight."

He peered over her shoulder at the bedside clock. "Seven twenty-five. Is that the right time, or is it several hours and minutes off?"

"It's accurate, but I don't care about swimming today." She slid her hand across his hip and kissed his shoulder. "I'd like to stay here and not come up until February. Maybe even March.

"Tempting," he admitted, "but I've got to get Colin and Darcy."

"Ugh," she groaned. "There it is. Reality."

"It doesn't just bite, does it?"

"You can say that again."

"How about meeting us for breakfast after you're done?"

Her smile was almost as bright as the one in her graduation photo. "I'd love to."

Chapter Eight

Glen hated leaving the warmth of her embrace for the cold of winter and the lonely drive over snow-covered roads to Jason and Sara's house. Everything about it felt wrong. Like the sun sparkling on the snowbanks wasn't as bright as it would be if she were in the car with him. Like the puffs of fog he produced every time he exhaled in the car's defrosting interior were wasted because she wasn't there to add her own to the atmosphere. He imagined the two of them steaming up the windows the way they had in the parking lot at the Chinese restaurant two weeks ago.

Was it only two weeks ago?

Last night had been phenomenal. He could live on a steady diet of her lovemaking and never want for any other form of sustenance. Yet as strong as the physical attraction was between them, there was something even stronger, and it grew with every conversation, every encounter. It was far more dangerous to him than fierce attraction because he had trusted his instincts once and been so wrong. He resisted putting a name to what he felt for Abby in case he was wrong again.

Jason didn't share his reservations.

"You can thank me any time," he said.

"Come again?" They were seated at the dining room table, waiting for the kids to get their outerwear on.

"For the introduction. Or maybe you need to thank Sara. After all, she's the one who sat you together at the reception."

From where she was bent over putting Cortland on his leash, she peered at the two of them through a fringe of auburn bangs. "I told you so."

"You told who what?" Glen asked.

"I told him you and the judge would hit it off."

"Both brilliant," Colin observed.

"Successful." This from Sara.

"Left-handed," Darcy added. "And single."

"Those characteristics don't necessarily lead to an attraction, though." Glen didn't know why he was arguing with them; maybe because he didn't want to be manipulated, and knowing his best friend's wife had played cupid felt a lot like that.

"When one of you is six and a half feet tall and the other one is less than five feet tall, one lean and narrow, the other pleasantly round? Of course, there will be an attraction."

Though Sara was right, it sounded much more clinical than what he felt for Abby.

"Don't argue with the woman." Jason scraped back his chair and took his coat from a peg by the door. "Remember, she's pregnant."

"Besides, she's right," Colin added. "When are you seeing her again?"

"We're meeting her for breakfast at Aunt Linda's place after she goes swimming."

"You're going to the Town Line Diner?" Sara's blue-green eyes gleamed with childlike excitement.

Jason interpreted her reaction for him. "She's got a *thing* for your sister's eggs Benedict lately."

"You want to join us?" Glen wasn't sure why he extended the invitation or if he even wanted to, but it was already out, and he couldn't take it back. He was afraid they might pick this conversation up where they left off but in front of Abby, and he didn't want her made uncomfortable. He was also jealous of his limited time with her and hated to share her with anyone else.

"We'd love to."

An hour later Abby came through the door of the diner on a gust of cold air, snow lying like crystals on her thick chestnut mane, cheeks glowing with remnants of her workout. He rose from his seat at a long table by the windows and crossed to the entry before he realized he was going to. He couldn't be in the same room with her and not want to be closer still.

Her gray-green eyes sparkled at his approach. She looked at him the way Sara looked at the diner's menu.

That obvious hunger sent a spike of lust through his blood stream. "Hi."

Her voice flipped a switch inside him. Crushing her to his chest, he leaned down for a kiss.

Abby returned his embrace, but when he stroked his tongue over her lips, seeking entry, she pressed her hands against his chest, exerting just enough pressure to make him take a step back.

"My reputation," she explained breathlessly, her color high, her gaze darting around the restaurant.

Of course. A small-town lawyer and judge in a public place, in a town where some people already suspected him of being overly sexed.

What was he thinking? The truth was he could hardly think at all when he was around her.

Then he didn't have to, because the kids waved her over to their table, and while she exchanged greetings with everyone, he got himself under control. At least until he took a seat beside her on the long wooden bench, their thighs touched, and the scent of her shampoo drifted up to him every time she shifted to take a sip of cinnamon herbal tea.

He was as witless as a teenaged boy experiencing his first infatuation. He ate but didn't taste his food. He participated in the conversation yet had no idea what it was about. The image of a white-tailed deer in rut kept flashing through his mind, though a stag probably had more control than he did at the moment.

"Man, have you got it bad," Jason murmured when they finished the meal and were putting their coats on in the entryway.

"Don't I know it."

****

"Carol of the Bells" started playing just as Abby finished cleaning beneath her kitchen sink. She hadn't seen the inside of that cabinet for at least two years, and it was everything she expected it to be. Dirty, damp, and full of things she must have thought she would use but never had, plus a few cleaning products that had expired when they were shoved to the back with each new purchase. Hearing the doorbell gave her an excuse to quit the project. She closed the cabinet doors and tossed her rubber gloves into the trash bag full of unwanted and undesirable items before going to see who it was.

Glen's bearded chin showed up in her peephole. She couldn't yank the door open soon enough, and she cursed the locks for what little delay they caused.

"I thought you were gone to New York," she said breathlessly, not caring if it sounded like she was excited to see him again so soon.

"Forgot something."

He shouldered his way into the room and kicked the door shut behind him. Abby's insides quivered when he dropped his hands to her hips and pushed her up against the entry panel. His coat was open, but he didn't remove it. He slid his hands beneath the hem of her shirt.

"And you think you'll find it there?" she smiled.

"Here." He pushed her bra up until the bottom strap reached her underarms, palming her breasts with cold hands. Ripples of sensation raced across her nerve endings and made her legs go weak. When one hand slipped beneath the waistband of her pull-on lounge pants and delved inside her panties, she went up on her toes. Her knees locked. She grasped his shoulders for balance even though she wasn't in danger of falling.

When his cold finger slid inside her, she bit the tendon at the side of his neck.

"Take me," he growled.

"Is that a question?" She laughed, because he added a second finger to the first and began a sensual assault of advance and retreat that was quickly turning her into a mindless ball of need.

"I'm not asking."

She almost came at the sound of his deep, authoritative voice.

He fumbled in his coat pocket with his free hand before letting the garment fall to the floor. His thumb pressed against her clit, and she pulled away from the pressure while at the same time he ripped a condom wrapper open with his teeth. She unzipped his jeans. Throbbing, pulsating against him, she didn't know if she could wait another second so when he stepped away from her and broke all contact, she cried out at the loss.

"Don't worry. I'm not done," he assured her, sheathing himself with the condom then reaching for her hips again. "But we're going into the living room."

We are?

Guiding her to the end of the cordovan leather sofa, he bent her over the arm until her torso fell across the cushions and her bottom was in the air. *Yes!* Her buttocks twitched in anticipation. Then he pulled her bottoms off and replaced them with his warm, hard thighs.

"Do you like this position?"

"I don't know, but I'm willing to find out."

With a half laugh, half groan he pushed inside her. One hand held her hips in place while the other played with her nipple, and she bucked against him.

"Too much?"

She gasped for breath, but managed to reply, "If you stop now, I might have to kill you."

"You sweet talker."

Then they ceased speaking at all, their bodies silently communicating with one another. His thrusts were hard and fast, and she reveled in it. She clenched her fists against the sofa and ground her cheek into the leather. Attempting to rise was futile. He pushed her back down and she silently thanked him when she realized the most intense feeling came from that position.

Harder. Faster. They rushed toward orgasm. *Harder. Faster.* It was a mantra in her head. Their height difference didn't matter like this. He could be five feet taller than she was instead of one and a half.

Harder. Faster. Yes! She was so close. Sweat pooled on her lower back and her hair tangled around her face. Scrambling with her left hand, she reached between them and stroked herself once. Her whole body convulsed. Almost coming out of her, he swore and clamped his hand around her middle to keep her close. She touched herself again, but this time she stroked him as he retreated, and felt his legs shake.

"You're killing me."

"Good." She didn't want to be the only one slowly dying here.

She stroked them both one more time.

He jerked back, bringing her halfway off the couch with him. His thighs went rigid, his breathing choppy at her ear, his arm a vise around her middle.

She grasped the base of his erection. He bit the nape of her neck. They both exploded.

It was wild and powerful, and the aftershocks continued until they collapsed against the sofa, doing their best to find a new rhythm for breathing.

Her bra cut into the skin at the top of her breasts. His shirt was rolled halfway up his torso. His jeans were twisted around his ankles.

"I'm going to miss you," he admitted into the silence.

"Hmmm. Me too."

Slowly he levered himself away from her body and righted his clothing. She tried to do the same, but a dizzy spell assailed her, and she fell sideways on her first attempt before getting her bearings on the second. The blood must have rushed to her head while she lay jackknifed over the arm of the sofa.

When they were both dressed again, she followed him to the door.

"Are we on for chess tomorrow night?" he asked, retrieving his coat from the floor. He put his hand into one pocket and withdrew a paper bag from the local pharmacy.

"Of course. I should be home at the usual time."

"For you." He held the bag out to her. When she took it, he pulled her into his arms and gave her the long kiss she wanted to indulge in back at the diner. The one that made her toes curl and tempted her to drag him into her bedroom and keep him there for days, nights, weeks. But he broke the kiss after a few minutes. "The kids are waiting for me."

Not until he left, and she had locked the door behind him, did she look inside the bag. His presumptuousness made her laugh out loud. His optimism warmed her heart. Inside the bag was an entire box of condoms.

****

Her dizzy spell returned later that night and again the next morning. Not good. Not normal for her, either, so she made an appointment with Doctor French at the general practice in town for after lunch. She had a client booked for that time slot, but one of the benefits of being self-employed was being able to rearrange her schedule when necessary. One of the downsides was she didn't get paid when she didn't work, so she needed to take care of this, whatever it was, before it got any worse and caused more cancellations.

"A sinus infection," Doctor French pronounced after a brief examination.

"I haven't had one in years," Abby said, "but I don't feel stuffy."

"It's possible to have one without that symptom being noticeable. Given your other symptoms and how long you've had them, it's safe to say this is bacterial. I'll write a prescription and send it over to the pharmacy for you."

Abby went home that night armed with a bottle of five antibiotic pills. Glen called within minutes of her taking the first dose.

Their conversation started out with the usual, "What time is it in Somerset today?"

"Ten oh six in the morning."

"I missed you last night."

"I slept with your smell all around me. In my bed. I can't wait to get under the covers again."

His laugh was a groan. "The things you say."

Eventually they talked about their Mondays, about her sinus infection and Darcy's upcoming appointment to go over lab results. They played chess for an hour, stopping only when Abby experienced a dizzy spell so severe, she couldn't bend over the game board any longer.

"I'm sorry, I guess I need to get some sleep and take care of this."

"No need to apologize."

"Hopefully it will be better tomorrow. They say these antibiotics act fast."

A few more exchanges about nothing very important and they were ready to end the call when he suddenly said, "Come to New York for the weekend."

"Okay."

"Okay?" He chuckled. "That was easy."

"Is that a bad thing? Should I have kept you waiting for an answer?"

"No. I like my women easy."

"Good." After a deliberate pause she added, "Because I like my men hard."

****

By the time she arrived on Friday night, she was wiped out. First there had been the two-hour drive down to White River Junction to catch the Greyhound bus going to New York City by way of four New Hampshire stops and a bus change in Boston. To say the trip was long was an understatement. Even with an audio book, a briefcase full of paperwork to read, her cell phone to play games on, and a book of crossword puzzles, she had trouble entertaining herself while traveling for ten hours.

None of that mattered when she saw Glen waiting for her at the station. Head and shoulders above the crowd, blue eyes searching only for her, he made every discomfort fade away.

She was probably beaming like a young girl deep in the throes of her first crush, but she didn't care. All she wanted was to throw herself into his arms and ignore the people around them.

Instead, she asked, "How on earth do you make that trip so often?"

"I don't." Grabbing her weekend bag by the strap, he put a hand on her waist and led her out of the Port Authority building where the bus station was located. "Lately I've had a little extra incentive to get up there."

"Flattery will get you...almost anything." She smiled, loving the feel of his lean body against hers and the masculine scent of his cologne. "Still, you must be exhausted by the time you get to Somerset."

"I drive it, which doesn't take as long. A little over six hours, but it's still miserable." He opened the door and waited for her to precede him out onto 42nd Street where he took her hand before continuing. "I used to go a few times a year; in July for a day or two of haying. Thanksgiving every other year when I had the kids, alternating with Christmas. A day or two in February for sapping. Maybe one other time if something special was going on."

He stopped at the edge of the sidewalk and, palming her cheek, dipped his head and kissed her. "I'm glad to see you, Abby." Pedestrians having to eddy around them cursed, the nicest comment being that they should get a room. A bitter wind cut through Abby's outerwear and despite his warm embrace, she shivered. Glen lifted his head and tucked her close to his side. "Let's get you home."

Ten minutes later they arrived at his condominium on West 56th Street. It was in an old building across from Carnegie Hall and close to Central Park with interesting architectural features and an elaborate security system. Above the main entrance the numbers 1926 were engraved in the stone arch to indicate the year of construction. Abby knew it was a pricey address even before he explained he had a three-bedroom corner unit.

"I hope you didn't mind taking a taxi," he said as he punched in the code for the door to his tenth-floor unit. "My car is in a parking garage, and I thought a cab would be quicker than going to get it, especially since I'd have to find a place to park down at Port Authority."

"The taxi was fine."

"I also didn't want you getting cold walking back to the car if I could avoid it. How are you feeling today? Antibiotics still working?"

"All better. I took my last dose on the train."

His concern touched her, but she didn't want to make small talk. There were only two things on her mind. One was making love to him; the other was sleeping. Since both involved her body being naked or nearly naked beside his body in the same condition, she didn't care which one came first. Well, okay, maybe she had a preference, but it was close.

Inside his unit, a small foyer gave way to a spacious living room with high-beamed ceiling and large, double windows on the far wall. He put their coats away in a closet by the door, then took her hand and said, "Let me give you the grand tour."

To the left of the foyer was a bedroom obviously used by Colin, surprisingly neat for a teenaged boy. The next bedroom, accessed off the living room, was without question Darcy's, and it was a mess. Between them was a shared bath. Also accessed from the living room was Glen's bedroom with its own bath tucked behind the small kitchen, which he could enter in the mornings through a connecting door.

Dropping her bag on the floor at the foot of his bed, he asked, "Do you need anything?"

An easy question to answer. "Just you."

He held his hands out in invitation. "I'm all yours."

Sinking against him and having his arms fold around her was like coming home. She clutched his waist and buried her face against his shirtfront. In only a short time his embrace was as welcoming, as comforting as hugs from her grandparents who she waited all year to see. She had only left Glen five days ago, but their separation felt as long as the months between visits to the islands and the delta.

A gentle finger nudged her chin up, and she looked into soft, blue eyes searching her own. "Are you okay, Abby?"

Emotion suddenly overwhelmed her. On the verge of tears, she swallowed the lump in her throat and simply nodded.

Glen pulled her close and simply held her. He didn't pet, just kept his arms around her and let her drown in his warm embrace. When she finally pulled herself together enough to speak, she leaned back and whispered, "Am I the only one a little overwhelmed by what's happening between us?"

Now it was Glen who communicated silently, with a single shake of his head.

She sighed with relief and laid her cheek against his chest once more. "Good."

Running his hand gently through her hair, he kissed her temple. "Would you like to go to bed now, Abby?"

"Mmm-hmmm."

Fifteen minutes later the travel, the beat of his heart beneath her ear, and the rightness of being with him all combined to send her into a deep sleep.

****

Waking the next morning, she rolled and stretched, basking in the warmth of his body curled around hers.

"Hello, Abby."

His voice had that husky, just-woke-up-and-haven't-had-coffee quality that made her want to purr like a kitten and beg to be stroked.

She opened her eyes and gazed into the slumberous blue of his. Soft. Direct. Lit with the same desire slowly pulsing to life inside her. Not wanting to disturb the moment, she kept her voice soft, a mere whisper of sound. "Good morning."

"Sleep well?"

She nodded. Rubbed her feet against his calves and sifted her fingers through the whorls of dark hair on his chest.

"What would you like to do today?"

Rolling onto him, she propped herself up with an elbow on each side of his head and kissed him, long and slow and with all the hunger she had banked that week while anticipating this time together.

"I want to explore every inch of you."

Reaching back, he adjusted the pillows, so he was propped up against the headboard. "Be my guest."

She touched, tasted, rubbed, and nuzzled every part of him until he was rock hard, and she was drunk on the pleasure of having him all to herself for an extended period of time. "I want to ride you," she said. A question. A confession.

His answer was a guttural, "Please."

Dragging her breasts against his torso, she lifted herself up until she was sitting on top of him, poised above his erection.

"Condom," he panted.

"Can we have one time without it?" She wanted to feel his heat, his hardness, his flesh without latex between them.

"Too risky." Regret echoed in his voice. The veins on the side of his neck stood out.

She rubbed her clit against his erection. "I promise I'm healthy and on birth control pills. You can trust me."

The pained look in his blue eyes told her that he wanted to.

"I swear on my Oath of Allegiance to the State of Vermont. I've never had sex without a condom, and I want this, us, to be special."

He surrendered on a groan. "Do it."

Abby sank onto his hard flesh. "Oh, that's good," she whispered, rocking against him. In her thirty-five years, she had never had sex like this, bare flesh against bare flesh.

Little tremors where their bodies met rippled out through her nervous system. "Touch me," she begged, afraid she might die from need if he didn't put his hands on her.

Instead, he surged up inside her. So deep her breath came in on a gasp and left on a gurgle of sound when he fell back to the bed and she followed him down, the movement drawing him in even deeper.

He did it again. Plunge and retreat. Plunge and retreat, until she found the rhythm and took over where he began, scraping her fingers across his chest and rolling her hips against his.

Her body filmed with sweat. Her nipples hardened to the point of pain.

He flicked one finger against a turgid peak, and a shower of sparks ignited inside her. Momentarily faltering, she drew a jagged breath, then ground herself against him.

Her head fell forward. She flung it back. Through glazed eyes she worshipped his male beauty while desperately hurtling toward a completion that seemed just out of reach.

He flicked both nipples and her stomach convulsed. Their breathing was erratic and loud in the room.

She changed the tempo, then changed it again when that didn't bring her any closer to orgasm.

"Want some help?" he whispered.

"Please."

Palming her breast with his right hand, he used the thumb of his left to stroke her clit. She swayed into the caress. He feathered his thumb against her lower belly, and she reeled back from the soft caress, too sensitive to endure it. Violent tremors wracked her frame.

"I want to watch you come for me," he said, and her eyes flew open to meet his gaze, direct, determined. He stroked her clit again, but this time he didn't stop. He circled the sensitive flesh again and again and lifted his hips from the bed.

When she folded over, he pulled her nipple into his mouth. One suckle, and her world exploded.

Lights flashed before her eyes. Breathing was a reflex action, one she barely noticed because the only thing that mattered was the blast of heat coming from him as he reached his own peak. It bathed her womb and seared her soul.

"Again," he said.

Again? She barely had time to process the word before he pulled her nipple between his lips and pushed down hard on her clit, and a second orgasm ripped through her body.

Chapter Nine

"I've never fainted before," Abby confessed, slowly coming awake in his arms. "Thank you."

Glen lifted her chin with two fingers until she met his gaze. "You are welcome."

They grinned at one another. He kissed her lips, her forehead. "Would you like a cup of cinnamon tea?"

Her gray-green eyes widened with surprise. "You have some?"

"I bought it for you. But we'll have to be quick because I get to choose our next activity."

Half an hour later they had showered, shared a large raisin bran muffin with sections of orange, and drank their respective hot beverages. Glen put their dishes in the dishwasher, then helped her down from the tall breakfast bar stool. "Time to get on with the rest of our day."

"What did you have in mind?" Abby followed him into the bedroom, her voice hopeful.

"None of that," he teased, because he wasn't against the idea of another round of lovemaking, but he had other plans. "I'm taking you to an undisclosed location."

"And what will you do to me there?" she grinned.

"Leave you."

"What?" That was obviously not the answer she expected. Dropping down on the side of his bed, she waited for an explanation.

"There's a pool at the gym where I play basketball. I don't want you to miss your daily laps, so I got a visitor's pass for you to swim while I get my own workout."

"Wow, Glen. That was thoughtful of you." She took his hand and kissed his palm. A simple act, but he wanted her to do it again, because it wasn't sexual. He needed the reassurance that she wanted him for more than just his body. "I didn't bring a swimsuit, though."

"No problem; I anticipated that."

Turning away, he pulled gear from a bag in the closet, and when he turned back with a maroon swim cap and black swimsuit with maroon trim dangling from his hand, she burst out laughing. Both items bore the Bates name and bobcat logo. "That was very naughty of you."

"I thought my alma mater might look good on you."

"You look good on me."

"And I'm going to again." He palmed the back of her head and pulled her close for a kiss. A brief one. "But right now, we're getting a different form of exercise."

They walked to the gym, buffeted by a brisk wind that sent Abby's hair into skyward-bound spirals. "Let me help," he said, catching it in his hands and smoothing it down into a makeshift ponytail. He tucked the ends beneath her coat collar. Then he wrapped one arm around her waist and brought her into the shelter of his body.

"I like the way you fit me," he admitted.

It was that simple. Mentally, emotionally, and physically, the two of them seemed made for one another.

Abby squeezed his hand, and he pulled the gym door open for her.

An hour later she emerged from the locker room , warm and damp, little ringlets escaping the heavy shawl of her chestnut hair and bouncing against her pinkened cheeks. Her long-sleeved T-shirt and yoga pants highlighted all her womanly curves. He could stand here and stare at her all day because nothing had ever looked so good to him as she did now.

"What are you so happy about?" she asked.

"You." If he looked like a teenager in love, well, he felt like one, and he wasn't ashamed to show it.

His reply didn't seem to bother her. Dangling the swimwear bag from the fingers of one hand, she reached up with the other and slid her fingers into the hair at the nape of his neck, exerting enough pressure to bring him down to her level for a sweet kiss. He had to get her away from Somerset more often if it meant she could show this kind of spontaneity in public.

A wolf whistle pierced the air and she jumped. Glen turned his head to see two guys from his basketball game leaning over the balcony above them.

"Hey, I thought you said she was a Mule!" Travis McCloskey called out.

"Yeah, but he's a bobcat," Skip Danahy added. "They're predators."

"True. I think this is mating season for them now, right? Hey, Plankey, don't bobcats mate in the winter?"

Instead of being embarrassed, Abby said, "Why don't you stop acting like animals and leave him alone so he can find out?"

"Oh, feisty."

"Better keep her, Plankey."

"I plan to."

Her body jerked, her gray-green eyes widening with surprise. Glen couldn't resist running his tongue across her pillowy soft lower lip. "Would you mind?" he murmured, kissing her cheek and then the shell of her ear. "If I kept you?"

She clutched his shirtfront between the open lapels of his jacket. "Just try and get rid of me."

They were both wearing dopey grins now.

"C'mon. Let's get out of here."

With a hand at her waist, he guided her to the front door where they zipped their coats and prepared to brave the New York winter. "Is there anything else you'd like to do today?" he asked.

"I want to go to a bookstore," she said without hesitation. "All we have at home to choose from is a wire rack in the supermarket or online shopping. I want to go to a real bookstore with so many shelves it could take hours to shop."

"How does eighteen miles of books sound?"

"Like a library."

"Nope. Three stories of new, used, and rare books to choose from. First editions. A whole section of nothing but books about music. And that's not counting the warehouse."

"Now that sounds like heaven."

"Then we're going to the East Village."

"This is it?" she asked when they stood on the corner of 12th and Broadway. Except for the maroon awning proclaiming the company name and purpose, Strand Bookstore might have been a hotel or apartment building.

"Trust me."

Inside, Abby spun around in a circle in the middle of the store like a child exploring a magical place.

"Like it?" he asked, already knowing the answer.

"I could get lost in here for a few days. Maybe weeks. All these words. It's like a fantasy come true."

"What do you want to see first?"

She screwed up her face as if pondering the question, gray-green eyes sparkling with mischief even as she stood on tiptoe and whispered in his ear, "You. Naked on the hardwood floor between the shelves with your favorite book draped over your...lap."

"I think I've found Miss Scarlett in the library." He murmured. "Now the question is, should she be armed with a candlestick or a rope?"

Her eyes flared. A little gasp escaped her lips.

"I think my woman likes a little kink," he teased, taking her hand. "Unfortunately, it will have to wait until we're alone. I've heard that delayed gratification requires...discipline."

When she closed her eyes, briefly, he knew she understood the word play and was turned on by it. Good, because he would hate to be the only one in this condition.

The rest of the day was spent like that. Deliberately brushing up against one another in risqué moves that might look innocent to bystanders but only heightened their state of arousal. Speaking in double entendres until even the most banal conversation became sexual foreplay. Petting and stroking one another into a near frenzy beneath the cover of a lap blanket while taking a sleigh ride in Central Park.

By the time they stumbled across the threshold of his home, they were locked in a heated kiss, groping at one another like teenagers on a first date. And like teenagers, they were caught in the act by the two people sitting on his living room sofa.

Darcy's mouth formed a big O of surprise while Colin folded his arms across his thin chest and smirked at them. Abby pulled out of Glen's embrace and hastily righted her coat.

"What are you two doing here?"

Darcy closed her mouth, her pretty face screwed up in a way that forecast imminent tears, and cried, "Mom wants to move to California!"

****

Abby watched all levity disappear from Glen's mouth as if wiped away by an eraser. He unsnapped his jacket and tossed it in the direction of the coat rack. Kicked off his boots and moved to the sofa where he scooped his daughter up and sat down with her on his lap. "Tell me."

Colin's humor had also vanished. Instead of a cocky teen, he looked scared and suddenly very, very young.

"Derek has been offered a job in Silicon Valley. It's a really good job with a lot of money, and Mom thinks it would be great to live where it's warm all year, so she's all for it, but she wants us to go too, and I don't want to leave everybody. I mean, it would be one thing to move to Vermont; we love Vermont and we'd be near your family, but California? I don't want to go to California! But can she make me, do I have to go with her or am I old enough to choose, because I can't remember what the rules of your divorce are, and I love Mom, but I don't want to go. You won't let her make us go, will you, Dad?"

"Breathe."

"But I don't want to go!" she sobbed.

Gently pushing her cheek against his shoulder, he kissed the top of her head. "Breathe, sweetheart. You're going to make yourself sick."

She took a deep breath as instructed, then began softly weeping into his shirtfront. He patted her back in a steady, calming rhythm and reached out with his other hand to squeeze Colin's shoulder. "You okay?"

"I don't want to go either," he said in a small voice that trembled. "Can she make us leave?"

Abby had been quietly hanging Glen's jacket up and righting his boots on the mat before taking off her winter gear. As much as she liked his kids, this was a personal matter, and she didn't want to intrude. They didn't seem to pay any attention to her as she padded softly toward his bedroom to give them privacy.

"Don't go."

His words stopped her. When she looked over her shoulder, blue eyes beseeched her to stay.

As unobtrusively as possible, she crossed to his easy chair and sank into the deep suede cushion, curling her legs up beneath her.

To his children he said, "Does your mom know you're here now?"

"No. We just told her what we thought about her plans and took off."

"We need to call her, then. So she won't worry about whether you're safe."

"Do we have to?"

"Yes." He reached into his pocket, looked to where his jacket hung by the door, then looked at Abby with a silent request. She retrieved the phone from his jacket pocket and carried it to him.

A few minutes later he had spoken with his ex-wife, whose shrill voice broadcast throughout the living room even though her words were indistinguishable.

Glen never lost his calm. He reassured her the kids were fine and told her they wanted to spend the night with him. When that didn't go over well, he reminded her the trains to Scarsdale on Saturday night were not a good place for them to be and promised to have them home first thing in the morning. Eventually she agreed, and they ended the call.

With that small victory Darcy brought herself under control and Colin visibly relaxed.

Glen opened the double doors below the coffee table and pulled out a game of Trivial Pursuit. "Why don't we show Abby what Saturday nights are like at our place?"

"I'm on your team," Darcy said.

"You're going down," her brother challenged.

It was a close game until the very end, but more than an hour later Glen and Darcy eked out a victory. "Two out of three?" Colin suggested.

His sister yawned.

"Not tonight." Glen put the pieces away in their plastic bag and folded the game board. "You two get ready for bed now."

They didn't argue, which impressed Abby. They thanked her for the game, and after brushing their teeth, wished her a good night along with their father. Almost like this was a normal situation they found themselves in. Which made her ask, when the two of them were settled beneath the covers and her head rested on his shoulder, "Do you have overnight guests a lot?"

"What?" He seemed distracted, taking a moment to process her question before answering. "No. I've never had a woman over when the kids are here. Why?"

Suffused with warmth from that information, she explained, "Well, they seemed to take it in stride. Don't you think that's odd for teenagers?"

He rolled to his side, so they were facing one another on the pillows. "I think they like you."

"Same here." The two of them were easy to like. In fact, if anyone had asked her if she got along with teenagers six months ago, she would have said no, because she didn't know any. She never expected to be in a relationship with a man who had two.

Glen ran his finger down the side of her cheek. "They know I wouldn't have you here if you weren't special."

Her heart warmed at the comment, but she kept her focus on his kids. "How is Darcy, by the way? Besides what happened tonight, is she feeling better now?"

"Yes, thanks." He feathered her eyebrow with the tips of his fingers, then played with the curls at the side of her forehead. "Her thyroid is off, so pretty much all her systems have been operating at half what they should be. The doctor put her on the pill to regulate her menstrual cycle, at least until the thyroid medication has a chance to start working."

"That's good news."

"Yeah. I'm worried about both of them, though. About what my ex-wife has planned."

That was only natural.

"You're a judge."

"I'm not a judge in New York," Abby said, gently discouraging this line of conversation.

"But you're a lawyer too. You know the law. Can she make them go, or can they choose where they want to live?"

Sighing, Abby rolled onto her back and stared up at the ceiling. She wasn't sure she wanted to offer any advice for fear of jeopardizing their relationship, but if the situation were reversed and her computer was hit by ransomware or some nasty virus, she wouldn't think twice about turning to him for help. And at least she knew how the courts in New York viewed these situations.

"There is no age. The judge will look at the kids' requests as an individual case and consider whether they are mature enough to know what they are asking for. A law guardian will work with them, assess the home life you can offer, weigh it against the home life she can offer, and decide what is in their best interests. Since you share custody now, even if they stay with you, they will probably have to spend considerable chunks of time with her. Like their summers and school breaks."

"I thought this would get easier," he admitted. "I thought we were done with courtrooms."

Unable to offer any words of comfort that wouldn't give him false hope, instead she reached over and squeezed his hand, letting him know he wasn't alone.

They fell asleep with their fingers intertwined.

****

She woke alone on Sunday morning. Slipping out of bed, she found Glen sitting in the living room with an acoustic guitar resting on his pajama-clad thighs, strumming *Here Comes the Sun* by the Beatles. His eyes were closed. She stood in the doorway, admiring the way the light from the kitchen windows glinted off his high cheekbones and burnished his dark hair.

When the last note faded, he lifted his head and opened his eyes.

"I love that song," she whispered.

He didn't speak but held out his hand. Abby padded across the room on bare feet and settled onto the sofa beside him. They exchanged a soft, relaxed smile, and he began another number.

"I usually play a song for the kids at night," he said softly so as not to disturb the melody. "My idea of a bedtime story. My mother used to sing this one to us at bedtime. It's one of their favorites."

"It's pretty," she said when he finished the tune. "What is it?"

" 'A la Claire Fontaine.' That's 'By the Clear Fountain' in English."

His pronunciation was beautiful. "You speak French?"

"French Canadian."

"Ah." The linguist in her understood immediately. "Not the same thing to a Parisian, I guess."

"Right."

He didn't talk about his family a lot, but when he did it was always with great affection. "Do you ever get to Quebec? To see your grandparents, I mean?"

He put the guitar back in its case. "Maybe once a year. I'll be up there a few times over the next six months for business, though, getting my nephew Trevor set up in a new office for the company. He loves New York and was hoping to work with me here, but because he's fluent in French Canadian, they want him there instead."

A wistful note had entered his voice. "You have a good life, Glen."

He shrugged.

"You don't think so?"

"It's fine," he said, sliding his pick into the guitar frets before closing the case. "It's good. Really."

"But?"

"But it's not the life I planned. That might sound self-pitying or something, I don't know, but all I wanted to do after college was go home to Somerset and work there. Be able to help my father and brother, raise my kids with Jason's son, spend time with my sister."

He sighed. "Instead, my ex-wife put an end to those dreams. I do have a good life, a really good life, and I'm not unhappy, but I wish I was here because I chose to be."

"You make it sound like all your life choices are already made for you. Like you're an old man and you'll never have any options again."

"Sorry." He shook his head. "That's just the stuff from this weekend talking. But my choices are made for me, at least for now. I think being able to see a few years into the future and knowing I can almost touch the time when I can finally choose my own destiny has made me nervous. Like if I don't grab it right now, it might slip through my fingers again."

"What will you do when that time comes?"

"I have no idea," he laughed.

"None?"

"None and a million. It's like I'm almost eighteen again. You know, when you have a dozen things you hope to be when you grow up, a dozen things you plan to do, and you haven't realized there's no way you can do all of them once you start on a path toward one."

"I do know." Once upon a time, she imagined having a houseful of children and a stimulating career. Instead, she ended up buried in a job that sapped all her energy and left her with no room for anything else. Having her name brought forward by the judicial nominating board and being confirmed by the governor to preside over the Essex County courthouse had been a godsend. She was too old to have a minivan full of kids, she knew that, but she could dream about a life of her own again. One involving a man. A child. Maybe this man's child?

"I gave up thinking about the future when I practiced law in Rutland," she admitted. "I just worked, all the time. That changed when I moved to the Northeast Kingdom. I finally started living again."

"Maybe Somerset holds the answer to both of our dreams."

They could have ended the conversation like that, but she would never be able to live with herself if she wasn't completely honest with him. "I think you might be the answer to my dreams."

It wasn't the declaration of love she wanted to make, but at the same time her feelings for him were clear. What he did with them would tell her if there was any possibility their future might be a shared one. So, when he gently brushed his lips across hers, trailed them to her ear and said, "You're not alone in that," she knew her trust in him was justified.

****

Glen couldn't wait to speak to her again. He settled the kids in at home with his ex-wife, found out what was going on with their stepfather's job offer, and called his lawyer. Then he took care of his weekend chores and waited hours that seemed like days while tracking Abby's bus online. Two hours after it arrived in White River Junction, he dialed her number.

"Miss me?" she teased.

"Always." He said without hesitation.

"Come to the Bahamas with me."

"Just say when."

"That was easy," she said, parroting his response from when she'd accepted his invitation to New York.

He laughed. "Don't expect me to say I like my women hard."

"I'm serious, though. I'm going to visit my grandparents, and I want you to meet them."

"Text me the details and I'll see if I can make it work."

****

Had he ever felt this way about Jillian? He couldn't remember. It was so long ago now, with other relationships and attempts at relationships in between, and the work and worry of everyday life dulling his senses, but when he was with Abby, he felt young. Carefree and optimistic about the future.

It worried him. Not because of her. In fact, he trusted her more than was logical after just a few months of knowing her, and that was what worried him most. His judgment had proved faulty before. Two kids, a messy divorce, a lifetime spent in partnership with a woman he couldn't stand, those were the results of that error. If he was wrong again, what would it cost him?

His soul.

That sounded melodramatic but didn't make it any less true. In just a short time she had become that important to him. Every night he looked forward to stretching out in his easy chair with only the lamp above the chessboard on while they talked and played for hours. It was better than sex. And the sex was fantastic. She was bold, adventurous, and comforting. The last was important to him. He didn't have to carry the weight of the world on his shoulders because he had someone to share it with now, and he wanted to do the same for her. Despite the lack of any vows between them, he would take care of her in sickness and in health.

Glancing at her in the airplane's executive pod across the aisle from his, he was glad he had upgraded their flights to business class. She didn't need the seven feet of space provided when the seat was reclined, as hers was now, but she looked a lot more comfortable than she would have been back in economy. Especially after lift-off when she was hit by a dizzy spell that had her running for the washroom.

"You need to see a doctor when we get there," he'd told her. Worried, because the sinus infection she'd had in January must not have completely cleared up and flying could exacerbate the problem. He didn't want her time here ruined by something a stronger dose of antibiotics could prevent.

He wanted her to be as relaxed as she was now, curled up beneath the complimentary blanket sleeping like a baby. She had been as excited as a child for this spring trip to the Bahamas. They only had five days, but with Trevor backing him up he was able to get the time off and planned to enjoy every carefree minute of it.

Before take-off Abby gave him the run-down on her grandparents, the islands, and her summers with them.

"They're called either Ms. Mutia and Mr. Robert or Ma and Pa. You should greet them with the first form of address, but they may tell you to use the second. Ma doesn't run the fruit stand anymore. My aunt Sabrina does, and Ma goes there just often enough to make them both think she's still in charge." She smiled fondly. "Aunt Sabrina is my father's little sister. Grampa sold his boat to my uncle Chris, her husband, and he's happy to let him run it without any help or interference. He'll make an exception for us, though."

"We're going fishing?" Now he was the one filled with anticipation. He thought they would just lie on the beach, which was fine, but some of his best memories were from summer fishing trips to the Finger Lakes with Jason. He still looked forward to that getaway each year.

"I have to keep my skills from getting rusty," Abby explained. "You know, as first mate."

Only now the first mate was out of commission.

"Can I get you anything else to make you more comfortable, sir?" their flight attendant asked, keeping her voice low so she wouldn't disturb Abby. He shook his head rather than reply. Abby seemed to react to his voice, even in sleep, and he didn't want her waking before she had to.

"I'll leave the immigration cards here with you, then. We should be landing in about half an hour, and they'll collect them from you when they stamp your passport."

Exactly thirty minutes later they deplaned in Nassau. Abby blinked herself awake just before landing, filled out her card, then sat with her face glued to the window. With his greater height, Glen could see over her head through the same pane of glass.

He took in the forested island marked by roads in a parallel and perpendicular design and the aquamarine color of the sea where it fell away from white sand beaches. A beautiful sight, yet most of his attention was on her. She was an independent woman, successful and confident, yet as they approached her second home, childlike excitement shone in her eyes. There was energy in her step, impatience bristling from her while their arrival was processed and the length of their stay noted on their passports.

"Almost there!"

She hurried along the blue, carpeted corridor, naming each fish in the tourist "windows" on the curving white walls, ignoring the glamorous advertisements for expensive cars and diamonds.

"Uncle Chris will be meeting us," she said after they cleared customs and baggage claims.

Outside in the warm, still afternoon, perspiration dampened the hair at his nape and trickled down his spine. Little chestnut ringlets popped to life at Abby's temples.

"Oh! There he is." She hurried past drivers standing among the white columns holding signs with visitor names, and went straight to a big bear of a man with dark folds of skin creasing bright, smiling eyes. He threw out his arms in welcome and Abby lunged into his embrace.

Glen thought the man might crack her spine with the strength of his hug, but she laughed and patted his face with her small hands.

"You got yourself a man, Miss Abby?" her uncle asked, raising his eyebrows and meeting Glen's gaze over her shoulder.

"You bet I do." Wriggling out of his hold, she snagged Glen by the elbow and brought him forward. "Uncle Chris, this is Glen Plankey. Glen, my Aunt Sabrina's husband, Mr. Merrill."

"Just Chris."

"Nice to meet you."

They shook hands. "This way."

Chris led, he and Abby chatting about family while Glen followed with their luggage.

Inside another terminal, Chris spoke to someone at the counter. "Just making sure our flight is all set," he explained, then they were out in the balmy afternoon again, crossing the tarmac behind the terminal to a single-engine aircraft with three passenger windows on each side. "Tommy is taking us," he said to Abby.

"My honorary uncle," she explained to Glen. "Dad's best friend growing up."

Tommy was as lean and light as Chris was hefty and dark, but he brandished the same smiling welcome, and he entertained them with island news during the fifteen-minute flight to the north end of Andros Island.

"Biggest island in the Bahamas," Abby told Glen. "But most of it doesn't have roads you can drive on."

"And the last big hurricane damaged a lot of those we do have," Chris added.

"It's still not fixed?"

"You know things move slow around here, Miss Abby. Then we had another round last fall."

Glen could see the damage before they landed. A ship lying broken on the beach, antenna bent at an awkward angle, with a hole as big as a door in its side. Palm trees snapped off halfway up the trunks, their dead fronds sweeping the ground. Creased vehicles and broken signs skewed across the landscape. Roofs of buildings hung drunkenly off the walls or collapsed in on themselves. "It reminds me of Vermont after Irene," he said.

"Hmmm. I was in Rutland then."

He understood her solemn tone. That city was in the worst hit part of the Vermont, and although there weren't a high number of deaths, in a state that small everyone knew someone who knew the victims and was affected by their loss.

"Now let's talk about happier things," Tommy suggested. "Like our little girl bringing a man to visit her Ma and Pa. This must mean something special. Right, Miss Abby?"

Chapter Ten

That wasn't the last time Abby's loved ones teased her. Glen heard story after story that night of Abby's youth, all told with fond indulgence. She was the apple of her grandparents' eye. Her grandmother talked almost non-stop, shaking her round little body and waving her hands to emphasize everything, but the subject was always the same: Abby. Her grandfather rarely spoke, inserting dry comments here and there in the best English tradition, but his blue eyes softened every time he looked at his granddaughter.

Aunt Sabrina plied them with fruit dishes, conch fritters, and rum until Glen didn't know what he was drunk on, but despite that he and Abby were up bright and early the next morning, joining her uncle at his skiff.

He greeted them with a big smile, as chipper as if he hadn't consumed quarts of alcohol along with the rest of them. "Let's go fight the bone fish."

It didn't take Glen long to understand why the other man used the word fight. He had never encountered such smart creatures. Every time they found milk in the water, indicating that the fish were burying their snouts in the silt and stirring up mud, the school moved on. If the wind shifted, they shifted too. It seemed crazy that they lived in just a few feet of water but were so difficult to catch.

When they moved farther from the shoreline, he could see the tails of the fish, but Chris explained that they were easily spooked. "Never cast your line too close to them or they swim away. You watch Miss Abby." He winked. "She's been doing this since she could walk. That's why I gave her the seven-weight rod, because she knows how to fight these things. You look strong enough, but I gave you a nine weight since this is your first time."

Glen wasn't insulted, especially when she was the first to catch one. Casting her line ten or fifteen feet away from the ripples in the water, she slowly, patiently, stripped it back toward the fish. When one took the bait, it swam away on an incredible burst of speed, but Abby reeled it quickly toward the boat.

"Shark and barracuda eat them," she said while Glen stood watching her skill with admiration. "That's why they're so fast, to avoid predators."

In the end she was victorious over the bonefish, and eventually he was too. They caught enough to make fish patties for supper before returning to her grandparents' home.

"I'll take care of the fish," her grandmother said. "You two go have some fun."

"Can we get to Andros Town by road?" Abby asked.

"Sure, sure. Borrow Pa's car."

"Thanks, Ma." She hugged the slightly shorter woman around her ample waist before taking Glen's hand and leading him outside.

She did that a lot. Took his hand, stroked his back, snuggled up against him. He loved her physically affectionate nature just as he loved her sharp mind and her sense of humor.

"One of the times it pays to be a lefty," she joked when they were heading down the east coast of the island in her grandfather's left-wheeled jeep on the left side of the road.

Glen laughed, enjoying himself as he hadn't done in years. It was a beautiful day, the top was down, and the warm breeze wafted over his body. Abby's hair was thrown back in a casual ponytail. Ringlets bounced around her forehead, the sun doing wonderful things for her golden skin. Wearing a tankini top and skort, she had him positively salivating.

"Are you thinking what I'm thinking?" she teased.

"Could be."

"I'm sorry about last night."

She had fallen asleep not long after they arrived, which surprised him after her nap on the plane, but not when he remembered she had been working long hours before this trip to make sure her clients were taken care of and her calendar was clear. Then there was the sinus infection.

"It's okay. I think the sleep did you good."

When she raised her eyebrows in question, he said, "You haven't had one dizzy spell today. Or at least, you haven't said anything."

She tilted her head to the side, appearing to give it some thought. "I guess I haven't. Maybe I just needed some good, hot island air to clear my head."

They didn't talk much after that, enjoying the warm day and the scenery, but when they passed a sign for Blue Holes National Park, he asked her what that was about.

"The island is full of blue holes," she said. "Underwater caves that can go down hundreds of feet, so the water in the center is dark blue and light around the shallow rims."

"Do people swim there?"

"Swim, dive. I avoid them, though."

"Why's that?"

"I don't like deep water."

Glen was surprised. She swam like a fish and was obviously at home on a boat.

"I need to see the sun, or I get claustrophobic," she explained. When he didn't comment, she said, "Maybe like you and public speaking?"

"Point taken." He had no trouble talking to people, any kind of people really, but put him in front of an audience and he almost passed out from fear.

"I can do it for a little while, like when I'm fishing because I'm concentrating on something, but I just don't understand people wanting to do it for fun. It doesn't help that I was raised on stories of the Lusca."

"What's that?"

"A sea monster, kind of like an octopus, that sucks children down into the blue holes out in the ocean."

He mock shuddered. "Why would anyone tell a child a story like that?"

"Kind of like the bogeyman? It keeps you from wandering off into the night, doesn't it?"

"Touché."

About an hour after leaving her grandparents' house, they arrived at Morgan's Bluff. While leading him through the caves, Abby explained that Captain Morgan used to lure ships there with a light only to have them crash against the reefs where he and his pirates could rob them. "I heard the story years ago but didn't know it was here," he remembered. "What ever happened to him?"

"He had a very successful career protecting the colonies for the British and died a natural death as lieutenant governor of Jamaica." She smiled. "And then they named a rum after him."

The caves and the point were fascinating when explored with someone who knew the area as well as she did. Glen was surprised by how few people they encountered, even on the rocky bluff with the amazing view. When they reached the top, they met a small group of tourists taking photographs. They didn't stay long. When the ocean crashed into the cliffs and spewed its angry froth all over them, drenching their cameras, they went away muttering that the salt probably ruined their equipment.

Glen didn't mind the water at all. It was a hot day, he wasn't carrying anything valuable, and the spray plastered Abby's little skort to her hips and thighs. Catching her ponytail in his hand, he pulled until she turned her face up to his. "I want to make love to you."

"What, here?" She laughed. "Now?"

"Anywhere." He kissed her breathless. "Now." He kissed her again while the ocean cascaded over them. "Maybe not here," he said. "How about up against one of those gumbo limbo trees?"

She wrinkled her nose. "Hermit crabs."

Two words that made him shudder.

Abby resumed their kiss. When she slid her hands into the back of his shorts and cupped his behind, he hardened against her.

"Where, then?"

She didn't answer.

Glen slipped his fingers beneath the hem of her tankini top and plucked at her nipples.

She gasped, then ground against him.

"I've been dying to have you all morning."

"You didn't say anything." Her voice was breathless. He continued playing with her breasts and she molded his flesh, pulling him close.

"That would have been hard, with your uncle watching."

"I think you're pretty hard." She smiled.

"And are you still easy?"

"For you." She stretched up on her toes and kissed his chin. "Always for you."

****

Abby lay sprawled naked across Glen's back. She stroked his calves with her feet and kissed his shoulder, the movements were lethargic. "I may never get up," she admitted.

Glen reached back and squeezed her thigh, his deep voice rumbling into the still afternoon. "Don't move on my account."

She kissed his shoulder again. Above them, a ceiling fan silently spun whorls of mildly cool air that barely touched their overheated bodies.

There was something about three days of swimming, lovemaking, and fish that rendered a person almost catatonic.

Two days ago, they made love on the white sand beach below Morgan's Bluff. Yesterday was a quick tryst in a cabana by the scuba shop where they rented snorkeling gear. But today was spent in Nassau with her cousin Aliyah, talking, shopping, and dining in a fancy restaurant, so they had to wait until they got back to her grandparents' house and a real bed before they could satisfy the lust that seemed to abate for a few hours only to come roaring back once they were alone again.

Would she ever get enough of this man? She couldn't imagine that happening.

Suddenly the bedroom door flew open, hitting the wall before bouncing half closed again, revealing her youngest brother standing in the gap.

"Oh my God." Hastily pulling the sheet up from where it lay twisted around her hips, she covered her breasts and rolled onto her side. "Romney, did you even think about knocking?"

"Nope." He gifted her with his devil-may-care smile, white teeth slashing in his too-handsome, dark face, and propped his shoulder against the door frame. "I heard the great spear fisherwoman was in town." His amused gaze took in the tangled sheets and bare skin. "How's it hanging, Glen?"

"*Tíngzhǐ!*" she almost shrieked, but while her face was hot with embarrassment, her brother's smile only widened.

"Shame on you, Romney," Ma scolded from the hallway. "Come and leave those two alone. You know how hard your sister works. She deserves this time alone with her man."

"Yes, Miz Mutia." He winked at Abby and offered a mock salute to Glen before pivoting on his heel and stepping out of the doorway.

Beside her Glen's shoulders shook with laughter.

Romney wasn't done yet. Ducking back into the bedroom, he said, "Spearfishing tomorrow."

"I'm not going deep."

"I wasn't talking to you, little sister."

Abby groaned.

Glen pulled her close to his side and kissed her messy curls. "You spear fish?"

"Sometimes. It's not my favorite type of fishing, though."

"Because it's deep?"

"Well, that and there are a lot of rules about it. You can't have scuba gear, so you have to be quick, have strong lungs, and be able to dive after your prey."

"Is it dangerous?"

"Not really. But you'll want to keep the lobster, or whatever you get, on the tip of the spear so if a shark comes for it, you don't lose your supper and your hand."

"Is that all?"

"There are a few other things to watch out for. Jellyfish. Lionfish. Red coral." She waved her fingers in an et cetera motion. It was hard to tell a non-native all the things that might be a concern.

"Maybe we can just observe?" he suggested, resting his forehead against hers. "After all, I do have kids to return to."

****

Those kids were waiting for him two days later when they stepped out of the elevator into the hall between their units. Colin was propped up against the windowsill. Darcy sat on the floor beside the door to Glen's condo.

He seemed as surprised to see them as Abby was. "What are you doing here?"

"We couldn't remember the code to get in," Darcy answered.

"No, I meant here, in Vermont."

"Derek got called to California for a final interview, and Mom went with him. Aunt Linda came and got us."

Glen tensed at that explanation, but his voice was calm when he spoke. "How long ago did this happen?"

"Saturday."

It was Monday afternoon.

"Have you been staying with your grandparents?"

Colin nodded.

"Then we'll go there to get your things, but tomorrow I'm taking you back to New York. I don't want you missing more school." He punched the code into the wall panel, opened the door, and waved the kids inside. "I'll be with you in a minute."

Abby waited across the hall in front of her unit. They had spent five wonderful days together and she had expected to have his company through this Wednesday, but that obviously wasn't happening now.

"I'm sorry about this," Glen sighed.

Resenting the change of plans would be like resenting his kids, whom she liked, so she opened her door and led him inside before speaking. "It's not your fault."

"I know, but I was looking forward to...well, more."

Abby didn't bother hanging her coat on the peg, instead going directly into the living room and sinking down onto the sofa.

"Does she pull stuff like this a lot?"

Glen nodded. "She likes to mess with my plans whenever she can. Put me in positions where I'll look like the bad guy if I react the way I want to, the way any normal person would react."

"I admire the way you don't rise to the bait." He shrugged, but she wanted him to know how special this was. Reaching for his hand, she waited until he joined her on the sofa before continuing. "My parents did some of that. Mom wanted absolute loyalty. She doesn't like David or Romney and made sure that I knew it. They knew it. She would have cut Dad out of the picture if she could have, and his family with him."

"That must have been tough."

"I love my mother, don't get me wrong, but I was a smart kid and logical, so I knew what was going on even if I didn't always understand it. You know, logos and pathos aren't always compatible."

He grinned tiredly. "You seem so balanced now. What helped you through it?"

"My grandparents. They were my role models, of what was right, and what unconditional love should look like. My mother is a feminist, so she always tries to prove that she is logical and rational and not guided by emotion, even when she's being irrational."

"Is your stepmother like that?"

"Flo? No. Her heart rules all her decisions. She's impulsive and warm and funny. Like Romney. She told me to scream at the top of my lungs if I needed to and bought me a punching bag."

"She sounds wonderful," he smiled. "Did you scream at the top of your lungs?"

"No. Because I could if I wanted to, and since I had permission, I didn't need to." Abby would always be grateful to Flo for that out, even if she never took it.

They fell silent, both staring sightlessly out the window at the late March sun hovering over the horizon.

Glen brushed his thumb across her fingers. The clock on the wall beside her grandmother's portrait chimed half past the hour.

Glen drew a heavy breath and slowly exhaled. "Would you like to have dinner with us?"

"I thought you were taking the kids to your parents' house?"

"I am. Would you like to come with us? Meet my folks and my brother Roger?"

"I'd love to."

****

The Plankey farm was almost literally over the river and through the woods from their condo. Across the road from Linda's Townline Diner, Glen turned onto a long gravel drive running between snow dusted hayfields.

"Have you ever been to a farm?" Darcy asked from the back seat.

"I've been to a few."

"I'll be you've never seen one like this. It's the best place on earth."

Glen followed the drive up a hill and through a break in the tree line at the top, and Abby could see why his children loved this place.

The two-story farmhouse, white clapboard with green shutters, sat at the front of the acreage, surrounded by a large network of pastures. A narrow shed connected the house to a long red barn the barn, and behind that, two silos caught the last rays of sun on their silver domes.

"Quintessential Vermont," she said.

"Home sweet home."

He was a lucky man to have grown up in this place. Abby would have loved one permanent home to call her own. Moving away must have gutted him.

"Come on. Mom can't wait to meet you."

"Wait, really?"

Her sudden nerves were unnecessary. Glen's father, a tall man with a receding hairline, nodded hello when they entered the kitchen, then handed her a knife and a bowl of steaming squash.

"That means you're in," Roger Plankey told her with a wink that reminded her of Glen. The blue eyes, she supposed, because the brothers were otherwise very different. Where Glen was tall and lean, Roger was just over medium height but square in both face and body. Linda was a combination of the two.

"Hello again," she greeted from where she buttered a pan of rolls at the end of the kitchen table. "Glad you could join us."

"Thank you." Abby picked up half a squash and immediately dropped it back into the bowl, hissing.

"Let me see." Glen took her steam scalded fingers and blew on the tips until they cooled. "I'll help." He snagged a long fork from a rack on the counter, speared a piece of squash and held it out to her. "You take the fork, I'll peel."

They finished one piece and started on another when Glen's mother joined them from the next room. Crossing to where they worked, she pulled her long dark hair into a ponytail before sliding an arm around Glen's middle.

"Maman," he said, "This is Abby."

"I see they didn't even give you time to take your coats off."

"It's okay."

"Well, if you're not too proud to help us make supper, we're happy to have you join our family."

Abby darted a quick look at Glen. A double entendre or an innocent welcome? His mother's first language was French, still evident in her soft vowels and the blunted edges of her consonants, so maybe she was only welcoming her to their table? Glen's only response was to kiss his mother's cheek and spear another piece of squash, so Abby took her cue from him.

"My mother likes you," he said when he came to say goodbye early the next morning.

"I'm glad."

"She and Roger's wife were close. Mindy. She died of breast cancer when Bryce was a baby, and we still miss her. My ex-wife was nothing like her."

Abby made no comment. Where Glen was careful not to say too much about the woman, especially around his children, she knew how much he had been hurt by her, so it was only natural that his family would dislike her for that alone.

"Anyway, I came to tell you that I had a great time in the Bahamas." Kissing her lips, he sifted a hand through her hair, still damp from the shower. "Thank you for sharing your family with me."

"You're welcome." She wanted to share more than those few days and nights. But were they on the same page, emotionally?

As if reading her mind, he pressed his forehead to hers. "We fit, Abby. You and me."

She could have joked about their sexual compatibility, but she knew that wasn't what he meant. Was he ready to make a commitment? Holding her breath, she waited anxiously for him to continue.

"Let's talk about that some more when I come back in two weeks."

"Okay."

Then he kissed her. A long kiss full of hope and promise. His hands warmed her body through the soft, pink fleece she wore, his scent surrounding her like a protective cloak while his tongue explored and committed her taste to memory.

When he let her go, she stumbled back.

"Whoa!" Reacting quickly, he grasped her elbows until she was steady on her feet.

"Sorry. Just a little dizzy."

"The sinus infection again?"

She grinned at him. "More likely it's you."

"I'm flattered. But if it happens again, promise me you'll see a doctor?"

She promised, then forgot about it when nothing else happened. Until the dizziness returned ten days later, and she made an appointment to see Dr. French.

The first thing she saw on stepping out of the general practice office was the church steeple on the other end of the common. Significant, since that's where she met Glen for the first time in fifteen years.

If Sara hadn't put them together at the reception, would they have ever talked? Argued? Discovered they were made for one another?

Abby squeezed her mittened hands together, almost bouncing down the walkway to her car. Could people on the sidewalk tell her secret? Was the glow she felt on the inside obvious to them?

A baby.

She wanted to announce it to the whole world, but Glen deserved to hear the news first.

Waiting for him to arrive was torture.

She cleaned the bathroom. Vacuumed the baseboards. Emptied the closet in the spare room and repacked it the same way again.

She wondered how he would react. Surprise, of course, but after that would he be as excited as she was?

He could come to prenatal appointments with her. Be in the hospital room when the baby was born. Play guitar lullabies at night to send it off to sleep, every night, seven nights a week, not just on alternating weekends.

She wanted to give him everything he was denied with Colin and Darcy; seeing the baby's first step, hearing the first word, watching presents being unwrapped on Christmas morning.

Hopefully it was a boy. Or a girl. She didn't care; she was so lucky to have conceived naturally at her age that she would be happy with either one. He probably wouldn't have a preference, anyway, since he already had a son and daughter.

What time was it? The clock on the wall said only nine thirty.

Maybe in the morning they could tell their families. They could meet Jason and Sara at the diner and share the news. They could get Romney on a video chat and tell him. Then there was Hume. He hadn't even met Hume! There were so many people on both sides to inform that they might not get to them all in one day.

She was still making her mental list when the elevator pinged. Having left her door ajar to hear it, she rushed out of her condo and met him at the door to his own. Laughing excitedly, she didn't give him a chance to remove his coat before pressing up against him and kissing him with all the joy in her heart.

"What is this all about?" he asked several moments later. "Not that I'm complaining, mind you."

"I have some big news!" The words flew out of her mouth the way a child would shout them.

"And are you going to share it with me?"

"I'm pregnant!"

Chapter Eleven

For two weeks, Glen had replayed his time with Abby, and he couldn't wait to get back to her.

She was smart. Sweet. Intelligent. Fun. He respected her intelligence and appreciated that she had a career of her own. In so many ways, she was his equal, and he imagined what their life together could look like. Going to the gym in the morning. Coming home from work, maybe having a glass of wine together, cooking in, or eating out. Playing chess before bed.

He still hadn't worked it all out, but the kids were almost done with school, and once they graduated, he could move out of the city. He felt free. Light. For the first time since his sophomore year of college, he could dream about the future.

Two words killed those dreams.

"I'm pregnant."

He froze.

Maybe he had misheard her, or this was a joke, and the punchline was still to come, but the wide smile on her face said that was a false hope.

She giggled like a schoolgirl and stroked his arm. "I know it's a surprise." She had the nerve to giggle again, like she wasn't destroying his life with her words. "I mean, you should have seen me when the doctor asked if there was any chance I could be pregnant. 'Of course not!' I said." She shrugged. "Guess there's no such thing as a sure thing, right?"

Glen finally found his voice, each word gravel scraping across his throat. "Repeat that."

Abby paused. The stupid, fake, I-have-a-secret-surprise! smile faded from her face, and she finally looked at him.

What she saw in his face must have finally clued her in, because she stopped petting his arm.

"Your hearing is fine."

Peeling her hand from his arm, one finger at a time, he took a step away from her.

The foot of distance between them may as well have been a canyon. He felt the loss, of her warmth, of what they had been building, of the trust he had put in her only to be fooled. Again.

Some men couldn't see past a pretty face to a woman's character. He thought he had learned from his own mistake, but here he was again, falling right into the same eighteen-year trap with his eyes wide open.

He couldn't look at her now. Spinning away, he stared blankly at the wall while choking on his grief.

"Glen?"

She sounded uncertain. Probably disappointed that her announcement wasn't going the way she expected it to. Welcome to the club, sweetheart.

"Hey. I know it's a shock, but you can talk to me."

He might have kept his emotions under control, but when her soft hand landed on his back, he went rigid. Fists clenched, grinding his molars, he turned around and shook himself free of her hand.

She paled but her gaze didn't waver. He had to give her credit for that. She was ballsy.

"Say something."

Cliché as it might be, and knowing she'd probably spin some unbelievable tale, he still had to ask, "How did this happen?"

In a matter-of-fact tone, she said, "I didn't know antibiotics interfered with the effectiveness of birth control. I took antibiotics for the sinus infection. Before the weekend in New York."

"Yes. I know when you took antibiotics," he bit out, "I'm not stupid."

"I never said you were."

No, but then she didn't have to. Her manipulative actions spoke for her.

"I find it hard to believe someone with your maturity and intelligence didn't read the prescription label." Sarcasm laced his every word. Her eyes narrowed, but he continued, "You know, they do have warning labels for a reason."

Her face flushed and her eyes sparked. "Yes, I know they do, but I haven't taken antibiotics since I was in college and had no reaction then," she snapped, then took a breath and continued in a carefully measured tone. "I don't take any other drugs, so it never occurred to me to read the label beyond dosing instructions."

"But you *were* taking another drug," he snarled. "At least that's the story you gave me."

"That does it." Pulling herself up as if she could add an inch to her minimal height, she poked him in the sternum. "You want truth?"

"I think I deserve it."

"I know your ex-wife lied to you, and tricked you, but if you think I'm cut from the same cloth, you don't know me at all."

As a comeback, it wasn't bad. A less gullible man might even buy it. Instead, he crossed his arms over his chest to keep from throttling her. Or, worse, reaching out for her because even though she had betrayed him, part of him ached for her.

Abby stepped back and turned toward her condo.

"Where are you going?" he demanded.

"Home." Not looking at him, she added, "When you're ready to talk to me without accusations, you know where to find me."

When the door closed behind her, Glen barely kept from howling with rage.

****

Righteous anger carried Abby across the hall to her own unit. She wanted to stay and fight, wanted to kick him or scratch his eyes out, but there would be no reasoning with him tonight.

He needed time to process. She got that.

Yet when the locks were set, the alarm engaged, she crumpled to the floor and dissolved into tears.

How dare he? Was his opinion of her so low that he thought she'd stoop to getting pregnant on purpose?

She could have sworn he knew her better than that, but now she wondered just how well she knew him.

Love could blind the smartest person. Maybe she had been the only one falling in love.

No. She refused to believe that. He just needed time. While she hours to get used to the idea, he was still absorbing the shock. Before long he'd be pounding on her door or ringing the doorbell.

He didn't come.

Eventually she got up from the floor and made it to the couch, alternating between crying her eyes out and mentally building her defense, yet all the time waiting for him to show up and make it better.

How pathetic was that?

When hours passed and she had moved from sorrow to anger to worry and exhaustion, she dragged herself into the bedroom.

So, it wasn't the reaction she hoped for; she would get over it. She wasn't the first woman to be questioned about contraception. But she might make him eat a little crow when he finally adjusted to the idea and came down off his high horse.

Until then, she toed off her shoes, flopped down on the bed without even pulling back the covers, and fell asleep.

****

Sometime during the night, she must have pulled the covers up over herself. She woke dressed in yesterday's clothes, bright sunshine flooding the bedroom telling her it was late even before she read the alarm clock; after eight.

Had Glen come over only for her to sleep through the doorbell? That thought had her catapulting out of bed, but a wave of nausea forced her to sit on the edge of the mattress until her head stopped spinning.

More slowly now, she rose and retrieved her cell phone. No green light indicated missed texts; no little red flag announced new voicemail messages. Tiptoeing to the front door, she opened it only to find the hall empty.

Still on his high horse, then.

Well, he knew her Saturday morning routine and where to find her. He had probably stayed up late, like her, and would show up after he rolled out of bed.

Yet when she finished her laps an hour later and climbed out of the pool, he wasn't standing on the concrete apron. His BMW wasn't parked beside her SUV in the high school parking lot. It wasn't in his space at their building either.

Nervous now, she went upstairs and took the quickest shower of her life with the curtain open, and her cell phone propped on the lid of the toilet so she wouldn't miss his incoming call.

Her phone never rang.

She took care of some research, read and replied to a few email messages, then made herself lunch, but the morning dragged on in silence and the afternoon yawned before her. Empty. Lonely.

Where *was* he? He should have at least calmed down enough to talk to her by now.

Part of her wanted to cross the hall and knock on his door, but she'd said she'd be waiting when he was ready. If she made the next move, she lost the moral high ground.

Usually that didn't matter to her. She had pride but not enough to be stubborn and stupid about it. Yet this was too important. It was up to him to make the next move and show her she wasn't alone in this.

David sent a text at three, reminding her that he was in Manchester for the day and wouldn't be back until after dinner service began at The

Gables. Romney was out of the country and didn't call. She didn't hear anything from Hume.

Or Glen.

He didn't call that day or the next. His parking spot remained empty. She checked it several times during the night, finally accepting that he must have gone back to New York without seeing her again.

Still, she justified his actions. He needed to be home, where things were normal, to come to grips with this new reality. It wasn't the future he planned, and she knew that would be tough for him to accept, but the man she loved would never reject their child.

So, she waited.

The week passed. Friday night came and went with no word from him. He didn't normally make the trip to Somerset two weekends in a row, but she had hoped.

When he hadn't called or sent a text message by Tuesday of the next week, she called him. Deliberately not dialing his number until nine at night because she knew he would be home by then, so if he didn't answer it meant he didn't want to.

Her whole body broke out in a sweat and nausea rose up in her throat, but she swallowed it back down while she listened to the ringtone in her ear. If she didn't pass out before he answered it would be a miracle.

The call went through to voicemail. Her stomach dropped and her heart rolled painfully in her chest. A beep signaled the end of her message recording time, yet she hadn't said a word.

Two nights later, Chief Charbonneau knocked on her door. "Hi Abby," he greeted, touching the brim of his peaked cap. "Sorry to bother you, but I'm here for a welfare check."

Had Glen cared enough to send the police, like Jason had last winter? Her heart swelled at the idea, deflated as soon as he continued.

"Someone was spotted trying to climb the fire escape to your unit," he explained. "Mind if I do a quick walk-through?"

"Of course not."

She followed him from room to room. He checked her balcony door, windows, and main door for risks. He offered a few tips about protecting herself and being aware of anything suspicious. When he asked about the condo across the hall, she told him there was an occasional resident.

"That's right, I forgot my cousin's son is staying here."

It seemed she couldn't escape Glen. Not when the planning board met on Wednesday, and she worked beside Jason whose careful conversation with her said as plainly as a billboard that he knew about her current situation. Not when she ran into Linda at the Aubuchon Hardware store while buying a new lock for her balcony door. Or when the chief rang on Saturday night to make sure nothing else had happened during the week to cause concern. He suggested she let Glen know about it so he could take steps to keep Darcy safe.

Right after that call, she drove up to The Gables. She needed her brother's company, and she could no longer put off telling him her news.

"Asshole." David rarely swore, but she reveled in his reaction. Proof that someone loved her.

"He'll get over it," she said, not sure if she still believed that or if she was trying to convince herself because the alternative was unthinkable. "He just needs time to come around."

Pulling her into his arms, David kissed the top of her head. "If he knows what's good for him, little sister, he'll get over it sooner rather than later. Any man would be an idiot to walk away from you."

"*Xie xie*. I needed that."

"*Wǒ ài nǐ*."

She loved him too. They might not be siblings by blood, but in all the ways that mattered they were family, and she needed her family's support right now.

Romney, of course, had a more emotional reaction when she relayed her news over the phone. "I'll hunt him down and castrate him for you. Just say the word." She laughed until she cried, but in the end, he promised to let her work it out. "Soon, though. My niece of nephew needs their father."

Hume, her Mississippi grandparents, and her father hadn't met Glen yet, so they assumed this was good news, and she didn't disabuse them of that notion.

Flo promised to start work on a pair of silk pajamas for the baby's homecoming.

Her mother was less than pleased.

"What were you thinking?" she demanded. "In this day and age, when there are so many birth control options. Don't tell me you planned this, or I will seriously question my name choice for you."

"No, I didn't plan it."

Her mother thought Abigail Adams was the original feminist and had named her for the long-dead president's wife. Hume was named for an Irish activist. In that moment Abby vowed to give her child a name born of love, not from some detached academic admiration.

"Well, there's no reason for you to ruin your life over it. You know what to do. And you can always come to Burlington, if you're worried about clients finding out."

A chill snaked down Abby's spine. She knew exactly what her mother was suggesting, and even though she hadn't expected any grandmotherly pride or joy in the news, she was still disappointed this option came so easily to her. "I'm not getting rid of the baby, Mom."

"Don't be an idiot. There are a lot of single mothers out there, but women no longer have to prove that they can do it all. I assume there is no man in your life? Anyway, it doesn't matter. There's nothing wrong with being a single professional woman nowadays."

"Yes, I am aware of that."

Her sarcasm went right over her mother's head. "Then come to Burlington. I can set the appointment up for you if you want."

"I repeat. I'm not getting rid of my baby."

"Fine! Call me when you've come to your senses."

****

Judge Henry was the last person she called.

"Congratulations," he said in his gruff, two-packs-of-cigarettes-a-day voice.

Abby's silence testified to her surprise.

"You're a good lawyer. A good judge. Better than me, I think, because you understand what the people in front of you are feeling and how hard it is for them to show up in court to end something that started out full of promise."

"Thank you." She could barely speak for the tears filling her eyes and clogging her throat. Her mentor had never said anything this personal to her before, and it touched her, especially given his feelings about marriage and family. His words went a long way toward making up for her mother's harsh response.

"Be happy, Abby. The law comes naturally to you, but you deserve more than just a legal career. You'll be a natural at this too."

But she questioned his judgment when, three weeks later, Glen still hadn't called or returned to his condo.

She found herself crying on a regular basis. Every time she ran into Sara at the grocery store or the post office and saw her happiness, the expectant glow that people gushed about evident on her face, she wanted to curl up in a dark corner. When she dodged questions from other pregnant women at the doctor's office about the baby's father and whether he was excited and what they had chosen for names, her heart broke all over again.

She resigned from the planning board. Seeing Jason even twice a month was too often because she couldn't take the concern in his eyes when he looked at her. He knew. Knew she was pregnant by Glen and rejected by him.

Her face broke out with acne for the first time since her teenage years. Her breasts, already large, were swollen like melons. They hurt if she slept the wrong way. Though her stomach was only slightly plump, and she could still hide her condition with her professional outfits, her swimsuit didn't fit, so she wore a bikini beneath a swim shirt but could no longer swim in the morning. It was too hard getting out of bed at that hour. Instead, she went in the afternoon or evening when the lanes were packed and a serious workout was difficult, sometimes impossible, to get.

An invitation for her fifteen-year class reunion arrived in her email inbox and later in the mail. She ignored the first but opened the second only to dissolve into tears when she read the details. To celebrate the June event her class would be facing off against rivals Bates and Bowdoin in a first of its kind Battle of the BBC academic and athletic games. Events were being held at all three schools.

It didn't matter that Glen wouldn't be there. She couldn't go and not think about him.

On learning about her pregnancy, she imagined a time in the future when their child would go off to college. To Bowdoin, of course, because there would be no way to choose between parental alma maters. She doubted she would ever visit Colby, Waterville, or the entire State of Maine again.

They wouldn't be missing anything. She looked like death warmed over. She was nauseous all the time, morning, noon, and night. She regularly fell asleep before eating, which was okay since she had no appetite, but not good for the baby. Her back hurt. Her waistline billowed out. Not enough for anyone to realize yet that she was pregnant, just enough for many of her clothes to be too tight. She looked and felt awful, and that made her mad as hell. If she had to suffer through this misery on her own, she was going to enjoy the results of it all by herself.

Her mother was right. She didn't need a man, especially one too pigheaded to listen, to even consider for a minute that she might not be as devious as his ex-wife and that maybe this baby hadn't been a part of her summer plans any more than it had been a part of his!

Resolved, she propped her feet up on the coffee table, turned on her laptop and did what she did best; crafted a legal document.

****

Glen waited for Abby to come to her senses. She must have realized by now that her story about the pill and antibiotics wasn't going to cut it with him. He just didn't know where they went from here.

Another eighteen years of being trapped by a woman stretched out in front of him. But he wasn't a college sophomore this time. He had experience with child rearing, child custody negotiations, and working with lawyers.

He was spending a lot of time in law offices lately. Derek's job in California wouldn't start until the end of summer, but his ex-wife had decided they should move now, at least she and his kids, so they could get settled in and meet people. That way school wouldn't be a difficult transition for them when the new semester began.

She assumed he was going to sit back and let her move his kids to the opposite coast. The battle between them in Guildhall all those years ago was nothing compared to what was happening now. This was all-out war. Just as Abby predicted, the kids would have to go before a judge and explain their own preferences, and they were assigned a law guardian to protect their rights.

He wished he could talk with her about it. On so many levels he resented what she had done but losing her as a sounding board and confidante hurt more than he expected it to.

"Call her," Colin said for what must be the tenth time that weekend as he drove the kids home to Scarsdale.

"No."

"Why not?"

"Just leave it. I have a lot of things on my mind, and some of them you wouldn't understand."

"Like her pregnancy?" Darcy piped in from the back seat.

He was so shocked his mind went blank and his body slack, his foot momentarily easing up on the gas pedal.

"Dad! Pay attention!"

Heeding his son's warning, he pulled himself together and concentrated on the road in front of him, but he couldn't ignore his daughter's question. "How did you know she was pregnant?"

"Trevor."

"Aunt Linda."

"Why would they tell you that?"

"We were worried about you. You've been acting weird, all distracted and grumpy. So, Colin said something to Trevor, who told him but said it was a secret, and I asked Aunt Linda if she knew about it."

"And she told you?" He couldn't believe his sister would be that indiscreet with a fourteen-year-old.

"No, but she didn't deny it. Same thing."

And he hadn't even told his best friend. Not face to face anyway. Instead, he'd waited until he got his temper under control, then left a voicemail message on Jason's phone. The next day he'd lost his own cell phone somewhere between New York and Sherbrooke when he made a quick two-day trip to check out the new offices there. He had a burner provided by the company while his history was being transferred to a replacement but losing it in the first place proved what the kids said. He was distracted. And grumpy.

He was also avoiding the conversation with Jason. He and Sara were responsible for him meeting Abby, and he didn't want to let them down. They were proud of their matchmaking skills. Both genuinely liked her. *I liked her too.*

"So, when is the due date?" Darcy asked.

He didn't know the exact date, but if he'd done his math correctly—he always did—she would be due in late September. It was mid-April now. "About five months."

"Oh."

He didn't have to guess the reason for the sad note in his daughter's voice. Darcy loved babies. If the judge didn't agree to let them stay with him during the school year, she would be in California when her little brother or sister was born.

God, what a mess. In only a few months he had gone from plodding through life to being excited about the future. From loneliness to hope to despair again. He had an office to open, a custody battle to win, a baby on the horizon, and the end of what promised to be the love of a lifetime. His head was spinning so much it hurt. Truly hurt, so when he got home from dropping the kids off, he took two Tylenol and went to bed.

As soon as he settled into the pillow his burner phone rang.

What now?

Aggravation showed in his tone when he answered with a curt, "Who is it?"

"Good to hear from you too, buddy."

Shit. He wouldn't have to call Jason after all.

"Are you going to talk, or should I just guess how you're doing?"

Glen sighed, making sure the other man heard it. "How'd you get this number?"

"Linda."

"Figures."

"Hey, *someone* didn't bother telling me his phone was out of commission. What else was I supposed to do when I called you back about your news and you didn't answer?"

"Sorry about that. I've been busy."

"Right." Doubt colored Jason's voice. "Since Abby didn't say anything at the planning board meeting, I take it this isn't exactly happy news for the two of you?"

"She set me up!"

"What the hell are you talking about?"

"She said she was on the pill, that's what I'm talking about. Said she had it covered. I still took precautions, you know, since I didn't want to end up in the same situation I was in before, but here I am again. With another woman who lied to me."

Silence greeted his explanation. Jason was good at silence. Glen couldn't stand it.

"Well? Don't you have some sage advice for me?"

More silence.

"Fine. Screw you, then."

"Dumbass."

"What did you say?"

"You heard me. I'll repeat it, though. You're being a dumbass."

Glen's head was splitting, but he couldn't take this conversation lying down. Tossing the comforter aside, he got to his feet and paced the floor beside the bed. "Why don't you explain that to me?"

"You think every woman is like *her*."

"Her, who?"

"Don't play stupid. You know exactly who I mean. Jillian." Jason was really pulling out the big guns, because they never used her name. "Not every woman thinks like your ex-wife. Abby doesn't. She's honest."

"Well, she lied to me about being on the pill."

"So, all the responsibility belongs to her? You didn't have something to do with it?"

I swear on my Oath of Allegiance to the State of Vermont. I've never had sex without a condom, and I want this, us, to be special.

He could hear her words as she begged him for one single time without protection. Remembered how good it had been, how it was like dying and going to heaven. Yes, he was responsible too, because he'd let lust overrule caution. Look where that got him.

"I don't know if she lied," Jason said, "but I've known her for a while now and would bet against it. More likely she made a mistake and missed a pill. Or it just wasn't effective. You do know they're not one hundred percent, right? And she isn't a young twenty something with predictable hormone levels."

"Maybe." He was tired, worried about a whole list of things, and he was the biggest concession he could make right now. His temples throbbed like a marching band had climbed inside his head. "I hear you. I do."

"But you're not listening."

"I'll give it some thought." He hoped that was enough to satisfy Jason so he could end the phone call and crawl under the comforter again.

Apparently, it was. "Well, that's something, at least."

Chapter Twelve

Two weeks later, Glen was so angry steam should be coming from his ears. He threw the mail across the floor of his living room, slammed the door closed, and when it popped open again from the force, body slammed it. The pain felt good. It didn't bring relief, but it gave him something to think about for a moment. Something other than the large manila envelope lying half beneath his easy chair. The one with the big bold letters spelling out *A. Wilson, Attorney at Law* just above the address. And what remained of the green postage ticket where the documents had been sent certified, return receipt requested.

Nothing about the envelope warned him of its contents. He had decided to buy the cottage in Somerset and thought she must be handling the real estate transaction. The last thing he expected to see were the words *Voluntary Termination of Parental Rights* heading up the pages of legal speak.

Even in his rage he could understand what the rest of the words meant, but Abby had enclosed a short note in her own handwriting in case it was too much for him.

If you want nothing to do with my pregnancy or the outcome, please sign these documents. One copy is for you, one should be sent back to me, and the third copy must be notarized and sent to the court in Guildhall. I've enclosed an envelope with their address as well as a bank check to cover the cost of filing.

As nasty as anything his ex-wife had ever sent to him. Worse, because it was so matter of fact, so impersonal, as if what they shared meant so little, she couldn't even be angry about it.

Well, he had no trouble with that emotion. It was roiling through his bloodstream and pounding at his temples.

Snatching the envelope up only to throw it against the wall, he cursed her with every profane word in his vocabulary.

It didn't matter that he had been seriously contemplating his conversation with Jason and was halfway to forgiving her.

She would not trap him! By God, he was not going to let another woman tie him to her for eighteen plus years. Taking almost half of what he made, forcing him to change his career plans, and preventing him from making any decisions without first checking with her. He couldn't change jobs because he carried the kids' health insurance. He couldn't move out of the city if it meant he would be outside a certain mile radius from her home. Traveling with the kids out of the country required him to sign so much paperwork that he stopped taking them to visit his grandparents in Quebec and instead they came to meet them in Vermont.

Not again. Abby was about to learn she could not dictate terms to him and simply expect him to go along with them.

He still had her number stored in his brain; there was no need for speed dial. It was seven o'clock on a Thursday night. She should be in unless her schedule had changed.

Her phone rang until it went to voicemail. He hung up and immediately dialed again with the same result. Half an hour later there was still no answer. Or half an hour after that.

He didn't get through until ten o'clock, and by that time he had worn a path in the carpet from pacing back and forth. He had also built up such a head of steam that the first words out of his mouth, unplanned, were "What the hell do you think you're doing?"

"Glen?"

She sounded groggy. He could picture her rolling out of bed, her body warm in that pink fleece she wore, hair mussed, gray-green eyes blinking slowly as she came awake.

"Well?" he barked, disturbed by that image and what it did to his body. "Would you care to explain this envelope I got from you?"

A long pause, then a much more alert Abby replied, "If you need clarification, I suggest you hire an attorney."

"I can read just fine!"

"Then what explanation is there?"

"Do you honestly expect me to sign off on my own kid?"

"Then, what is it you *do* want? Because you've made it clear you don't want anything to do with this child. *Or me.*"

"I want you to admit that you tricked me! Put that in writing and send it certified, return receipt requested. Then we'll talk about parental rights."

****

Glen's head hadn't stopped spinning for weeks.

When Darcy took her first step, he wasn't there to see it. When Colin went to preschool, he lived in another town, his ex-wife having moved with the kids to Scarsdale and set up house with the first of many live-in boyfriends.

Glen wasn't there in the middle of the night to comfort his children when they were sick. He didn't put money under their pillow when they lost a tooth.

Over the years he did the best job he could. The kids wanting to stay with him instead of moving to California with their mother proved he was a good father. He worked, year in and year out, at being a constant source of love and security in their lives.

What will Abby's child have? The question slipped in like a serpent, coiling around his thoughts and twisting his emotions.

He would be there for Abby's child. There was never any doubt about that, despite the way this came about. He couldn't walk away from this baby any more than he could have walked away from Colin and Darcy. But again, he wouldn't be there full time.

There would be uncles, of course. Maybe some other male figure. It would be hard for any man to resist a woman like that. Confident. Smart. Sexy.

A chill rippled down his spine.

The idea of any man living with her, sleeping in her bed, raising their child, brought sweat to his brow.

He had never cared about another man being with his ex-wife. In the beginning her relationships were an affront to his pride. With the longer ones, he'd worried about the men treating his children well, but there was no jealousy.

The thought of Abby with another man made his blood run cold.

Did it matter if she'd tricked him? Was it even true? He couldn't remember Darcy's doctor warning them about birth control and antibiotics. Abby was a brilliant woman, but that didn't make her infallible. She'd probably read the directions on the package, not the tiny print, multi-page insert from the pharmacy where warnings like that were listed. He was a genius, yet he'd been duped by his first wife. Too confident in his own rational mind to listen when his college friends warned him about her. By the time he introduced her to Jason, who saw through her immediately, it was too late. Colin was already on the way.

His chest hurt. His brain spun. Dropping into the easy chair, he put his head between his knees and sucked in air, but deep breathing didn't help. He could not trust his own judgment where Abby was concerned. He wanted so badly to believe her.

What if he was wrong, and she wasn't trustworthy?

Worse, what if she was everything she claimed to be, and he had abandoned her?

On the verge of passing out, he reached blindly for his cell phone on the end table.

Speed dial was made for times like this. He punched in three keys and waited for the ring tone. When it rang and rang without answer, panic squeezed the air from his lungs, and he stumbled out of his chair to lay on the carpet.

His heart raced. The room spun in a blur. Would anyone find him if he had a heart attack right here, right now? He didn't want his kids walking in to find his stiff corpse at the end of the weekend.

"Are you there, or is this a pocket dial?"

Jason's voice. He must have already answered the phone and received no response.

Gasping, Glen rolled onto his side and clutched the phone like a lifeline. "I'm here," he croaked.

This was more terrifying than public speaking. He had only experienced this kind of panic in the courtroom sixteen years ago, when he listened while his ex-wife annihilated his character and put his rights as a father at risk. This was so much worse.

"Glen? What's wrong?"

His answer was a cry from the depths of his soul. "I'm in trouble."

****

"Do you want this woman?" Jason had asked when he finally got his panic attack under control.

"I think that's pretty obvious, given the situation."

"Not like that. I mean, would you want her if there was no child?"

"Yes." No hesitation there.

"So, you're crazy about a woman who is crazy about you, and she just happens to be carrying your baby."

"Unplanned baby."

"Irrelevant."

Was it really that simple? Didn't he already know the answer without his best friend pointing it out to him?

He missed her every day. He missed their phone calls, their chess games, everything about her. The real question was, what was he going to do about it?

He couldn't just call her and say, "Sorry, my bad." Not only would that insult her intelligence, but she probably wouldn't believe him.

Making and sending a video to her was a start. Enlisting the help of friends and family was next. He had everyone watching out for her, even though she didn't know it, until he could be there himself. In the meantime, he worked like a madman to get his life in order.

The judge ruled in his favor, but the kids would have to go with their mother from mid-July to the end of August this year, then every summer until they came of age. Thanksgiving and Christmas holidays would alternate as they always had. February vacation was with her, April vacation with him. It was as ideal as shared custody could get.

Every two or three days he flew to Sherbrooke to get the Quebec office up and running. When he was in New York, he worked late into the night on the same, training his nephew Trevor in all aspects of his job. At the end of June, the new office went live, and he was either on site overseeing operations or at the Toronto Exchange.

He hated being away, but he was doing it for Abby, for their future. She deserved to have his undivided attention when he came to her. She also deserved a phone call.

He tried to reach her on Friday night but got no answer. Despite her previous habits, she might already be asleep. On Saturday night he called earlier with the same result. Was she ignoring his call? While she could be forgiven for that after what he'd put her through, it wasn't like Abby to back down from a fight, so he tried again on Sunday. When her sweet voice came on the line, he sank onto the bed in his hotel room, momentarily speechless with longing.

****

Unreasonable ass, Abby thought before he disconnected that last call. She wished she had done it first or, better yet, been talking to him on a landline so she could have slammed it down in his ear. Instead, she made do with a text message to the number he called from. *You have thirty days.*

The deadline was already on the paperwork but reminding him gave her the last word.

Not that it made her feel any better. Even her anger was temporary, replaced almost immediately by the depression that plagued her since she told him about her pregnancy. Fatigue made her life difficult, but his rejection made it miserable.

The morning after that argument, her cell phone rang at the office. Her family knew better than to disturb her at work, so her first thought was that Glen was calling to apologize.

Instead, it was Doctor French.

"Hi, Doc," she greeted, anxious because it was the physician herself and not a member of her staff.

"I'm calling to see if you can come into the office this afternoon?"

Uh-oh. Anxiety turned into fear.

"It's nothing to worry about," the doctor said as if reading her mind, "but I was looking at your numbers from Monday's appointment, and your weight gain is higher than expected at this stage of your pregnancy. It may be nothing, just a big baby, but I don't want to take any chances. If you can come in, we'll double check your sugar and blood pressure and maybe do another ultrasound."

Hours later Abby stumbled out of the examination room and plopped down onto one of the chairs in the reception area.

A toddler pushed a plastic dump truck past her feet and made a *vroom* noise. She barely noticed. The bell above the door jingled as another patient entered. She didn't even look up.

"Would you like some water?"

The question only registered when a paper cup came into her line of vision. She lifted her gaze to find the receptionist smiling sympathetically and urging her to take the cup.

Abby swallowed the contents in one gulp.

The receptionist laughed. "You looked like you could use that. It isn't every day a woman finds out she's having twins."

Abby started to thank her for her thoughtfulness, but the words died on her lips because the new patient standing at the window behind her was tall and attractive, with gray-streaked dark hair. Glen's mother. The O on that woman's lips said she had heard every word.

****

Abby dragged herself out of the elevator and stumbled across the foyer to her condo door. Tonight, she only swam half an hour at her usual pace before fatigue set in, and she couldn't wait to flop down on the nearest soft surface.

Unfortunately, her sofa was out. Random articles of clothing were draped over the arms and back, and her half-filled suitcase lay spread open on the cushions, waiting for her to finish packing for a weekend conference.

Her comfortable padded chair, made special for her height, was not even a consideration. She couldn't look at it because the little table beside it held her chess board. She should put it away, but the idea of ending that game for good was too painful, so instead she left it there, untouched and accumulating dust, a daily reminder of her situation.

Her bed wasn't made. What was the point? Stacks of papers dominated one side and piles of clean laundry covered the foot of the comforter. She didn't bother to move them, just kicked off her shoes and collapsed onto the welcoming surface.

She had barely closed her eyes when her phone jingled to indicate an incoming text. That was unusual. Few people knew her number, even fewer called it, and none of her family members sent texts. Her brothers claimed they were afraid she'd accidentally delete the message, though she never had. Yet it must be one of them, and if she didn't answer now, she'd just get a call later.

Rolling to the edge of the mattress, she rummaged blindly through her bag where it lay on the floor until her hand closed over the smooth rectangular instrument. Raising it to eye level, she squinted at the panel then almost dropped it on seeing Glen's name as the sender.

She was wide awake now.

The man could destroy her with one line, especially if that line was *it's over*.

He could also save her if the words were *I'm sorry*.

Perspiration dotted her forehead.

Incapable of deciding whether to read the message tonight or leave it for later, she retrieved the all-important die from her nightstand. If it landed on an odd number, she would read the message. If even, she would go to sleep—as if she could sleep now—and read it in the morning.

Rolling the die across the tabletop, she waited breathlessly for it to come to a stop.

Three black dots on the white cube.

With shaking hands, she put it back in the drawer. Propping herself up against the headboard, she took a deep breath, and opened his message.

It was a video. Warier than ever now, she pushed the little triangle for play.

He was in the living room of his New York condominium. Behind him an orange and pink sky filtered through the cracked blinds, throwing him into stark relief. His hair was disheveled, his beard a little longer than usual, his eyes ringed with fatigue. Was he as worn out as her, or was that a trick of the light?

"Abby, here is your answer," he said, holding a fistful of papers up close to the camera. Close enough for her to read the title, *Voluntary Termination of Parental Rights*. She held her breath waiting for him to flip through the pages and show his signature on the last one. Instead, he moved the document away from the lens and held up a candle lighter. Slowly, eyes steady on the camera as if looking directly at her, he put the lighter to the bottom corner of the pages and flicked the switch. Flames took hold of the paper and licked their way up the side.

"I'll be up this weekend." He dropped the pages onto a glass plate on the coffee table and let them burn. "I hope you're ready for a long talk."

The video ended.

Abby stared at her telephone until the screen went black and reflected her own image back at her.

He hadn't denied paternity, but that wasn't the same as wanting her back. His *long talk* could be about shared custody or about the two of them. It could be about starting over or ending their relationship once and for all.

With unsteady fingers she brought her screen back to life and wrote a reply to his text. She accidentally deleted it while trying to make edits-her brothers would laugh at that- and had to start over. Four revisions later she finally sent a message simply saying, *I'm flying to DC on Friday for a conference and won't be home until Monday. Call me.*

Her phone was silent all night.

With no missed calls the next day, or the one after that, her anxiety returned and with it her depression. By the time she finished packing for her flight on Friday, she was upset but glad to put some distance between herself and the empty condo across the hall.

Mercifully nothing about her flight made the news, and she returned Monday night in one piece but so tired she almost tripped over the fruit basket outside her door.

Picking it up, she found a card attached to the green cellophane with her name written in bold block letters. There was no further identification. No sender's name, no company, but since the entire selection was native to Andros, she called Romney to thank him.

"Wasn't me, little sister."

"C'mon. Who else knows all my favorites?" She poked the eyes out of the coconut and drained the milk into a glass. "There's even sour orange in here."

"Don't know what to tell you. But I'll be flying in from Paris Thursday night if you want to save me some."

"Not a chance."

She cored the pineapple before calling David but got the same response.

Briefly she wondered if Glen was the sender, then dismissed the idea. If he couldn't even call her, he was unlikely to send her a gift.

In the end it didn't matter who the fruit came from. She filled a mixing bowl with pineapple, coconut, Persian lime, and mango and ate the whole thing.

****

"Carol of the Bells" woke her the next morning, but when she went to the door, the hall was empty. A brown paper bag was on the floor at her feet with her name printed in bold block letters on the folded top.

Cautiously lifting it, she almost moaned when the scent of freshly baked yeast and cinnamon wafted from inside, stimulating her appetite as nothing had since her pregnancy began. She couldn't close the door fast enough.

At her kitchen table she wolfed down the large cinnamon bun, licked the sticky sweet residue from her fingers, and gave a happy sigh, feeling almost human for the first time in months.

A second bag showed up Wednesday morning. She took her time with this one, pulling the roll apart and eating the sections slowly to make the experience last.

On Thursday she put the cinnamon bun on a plate with sliced mango, filled a tall glass with milk, and made a whole meal of it.

Yet another surprise waited for her when she came home from her swim that evening. Jason and Sara stood beneath the shade of a maple tree separating her parking spot from the river below. Two bicycles were propped against the tree trunk and helmets dangled from their hands.

Abby wished a little resentfully that Sara was bigger. The younger woman carried her baby like a basketball was stuffed under her shirt, while she had to slide her seat back as far as it would go to get out from behind the steering wheel.

Jason hurried over to give her a hand. "We're here to make supper," he said.

"My kitchen's a mess."

"We'll figure it out."

Upstairs in her condo she hurried to clear enough counter space for them to unpack the contents of the grocery bag they brought. She hadn't been kidding about the mess. The place wasn't dirty, just cluttered.

"I know you love fish, but the smell makes Sara nauseous," Jason said, "so we brought steak."

"What can I do?"

"Keep us company," Sara smiled.

She missed Glen every day, all day long, but she hadn't realized how much she missed simple conversation with others until tonight. It was also a pleasure to watch the two of them work, touching every time they came close to one another. Abby couldn't even be jealous when she knew how long Jason had waited for Sara to come into his life. Especially not when they served the meal; thin broiled steak covered in tomato kiwi salsa and angel hair pasta tossed with olive oil, fresh parmesan cheese, and small cuts of asparagus.

"Oh my gosh," she groaned after the first few mouthfuls. "Do you two cater?"

****

By the weekend she wondered if there was a secret campaign to keep her from being alone. David and Romney showed up at her office on

Friday afternoon and announced they were going to clean her condo. When she went upstairs after work, the place was spotless.

Romney sprawled across her sofa in that carefree, boneless way of his as if he hadn't spent the last two hours toiling through her mess.

"Where's David?" she asked.

"Gone back to The Gables to get ready for dinner service." Rolling to an upright position, he said, "By the way, you're invited to a baby shower there next Saturday."

"I am?"

"Jason asked David to pass the invitation along, so I'm the third hand messenger."

"It's for Sara, then?"

"Yep. One o'clock sharp. Big brother is letting them use the back dining room for it. He told Sara he needed a piano player for a special function to get her there."

She was debating whether she should go or find a way to politely decline when Romney leveled his coffee-colored gaze on her and said, "Don't even think about it. He was your friend before Glen came along."

She shrugged an acknowledgment. "He's still my friend." Remembering the scrumptious meal they made, she added, "They both are."

"Good. Then why don't you get ready for the pool? I brought my swim trunks to join you. Then we can drive down to St. Johnsbury and look for a shower gift."

They were in the Green Mountain Mall when her phone rang. Though there were few shoppers, she moved out of the traffic lane and leaned against the wall beside the Northeast Kingdom Chamber of Commerce office to see who it was. The overhead lights glared against the screen, making it difficult to read the number, but the identity was clear: *wireless caller*.

She ignored it only to get another call the following evening. Probably some telemarketing company that slipped through her do-not-call lists.

Yet when *wireless caller* showed up again on Sunday night, she answered the phone. It was after nine. That meant it couldn't be an aggressive sales call and was probably just a wrong number.

She was sure of it when she answered only to be met with silence.

Was it the creeper? A chill snaked down her spine, quickly followed by anger. She wouldn't let some dirtbag intimidate her.

"Look, I don't know who this is—"

"It's me, Abby."

Tears filled her eyes and splashed onto the paperwork spread across her knees. Legal speak turned into ink blots. The empty space inside her, created by his rejection, throbbed with pain as hope rose like a volcano, and she tried to tamp it down out of self-preservation.

"How are you feeling?"

She swallowed. "Fine." A croak. A lie.

"Really?"

No. I'm not me without you. "Yes. Just tired."

His voice dropped an octave. "I've been worried about you." His words in that lower register rippled through her veins like Bahamian sunshine.

He wasn't apologizing for not getting in touch sooner. She wouldn't apologize for being pregnant.

"Is this really why you called?" she finally whispered, needing to know if this was about them, or the situation. "To see how the pregnant lady is faring?"

"I do care about the baby." He sighed, and she could picture him closing his beautiful blue eyes, dark curls falling across his brow as he bent his head with worry. She wanted to smooth that hair back and soothe him with her touch. How pathetic.

"I do care," he repeated. "In spite of how I reacted, this is my child, too."

She believed him, but what now?

"Will you be around on the Fourth of July? I'm coming up to help Roger with the haying."

A week from now. Her belly tumbled with nervous anticipation, reducing her answer to a single syllable. "Yes."

"Let's talk then. Face to face."

"Okay."

She finally had the man on the phone, willing to discuss their future, and she couldn't even form a complex sentence.

"Abby?"

"Yes?"

"I do care about the baby."

She really never doubted that he would. Not once he got over his initial anger. "I know."

"But it's you I've been worried about. Always you."

Chapter Thirteen

Glen was in the middle of a video conference call between the Toronto Exchange, Montreal Exchange, and Sherbrooke office Monday afternoon when Darcy called. He knew it wasn't an emergency or she would text their code; two days, nine hours less six minutes from the time at home. He had shared it with the kids before leaving on his first trip to Canada.

"How'd you come up with that?" Colin had asked.

"It's Abby's code. Our code."

"You're a lost cause," he lamented.

"I think it's wonderful," Darcy enthused. "Soooo romantic. And sweet."

"You're sweet," he said. His daughter was turning into a sensitive young woman with a generous nature, and he was proud of her. But when he finally returned her call that evening, she was a panicked child again.

"Oh my God, Dad, I blew it! I'm so sorry."

"Slow down. I'm sure it's not the end of the world."

"But that's just it! I went to see Abby today, and I really screwed up."

Sitting up straight now, then standing because he couldn't sit, he paced the few feet between his bed and the hotel room door, wondering what catastrophe had taken place.

"Dad?"

Darcy's small, scared voice begged for reassurance.

"It's okay. I'm sure that whatever you did it can't be that bad." He wasn't sure of any such thing.

"But I told her about the cinnamon buns!"

Was that all? Relief made him sag against the door. "Why don't you take a deep breath, slow down, and tell me what happened."

She inhaled so forcefully he could hear it over the line, and her story came out on a rush of exhaled air. "I went to Abby's office to take her a cinnamon tea. It was late, because Linda got a rush at the diner this morning, and someone called in sick, and she couldn't send anybody over with the cinnamon bun today. I said I'd go, and she told me to get a cinnamon tea from The Common Store since you said Abby likes them, and since it was too late for breakfast anyway. Well, anyway, I was just supposed to give her the tea and maybe say hi, but I blurted the whole thing out when she said it was thoughtful of me to stop by and bring her a drink. I told her about Aunt Linda being busy, and about how you asked her to deliver a cinnamon bun to her each morning until you could do it yourself and…" Darcy's voice petered out as she ran out of air. "I'm sorry, Dad. I didn't mean to tell her."

It was such a forlorn apology he had to forgive her. "It's okay, sweetheart."

"But I know you wanted it to be a secret. Colin's right. I can't keep my mouth shut."

Leave it to her brother to say that. "Don't worry about it. The secret isn't as important as Abby being taken care of. I'm sure you were just excited to see her."

"Oh. My. God. I forgot the best part!"

He laughed again. Darcy's enthusiasm was hard to resist. Ever since she was a little girl, her stories were rushed and full of emotion. She said she only had two days a week to tell him seven days' worth of news.

"What was the best part?"

"Abby loves the cinnamon buns, by the way."

"That's it?"

"No, of course not. I just didn't want to forget. She said they're the best ones she's ever tasted, and she eats breakfast now that she gets them, because before she didn't feel like eating in the morning, you know, because of the baby and everything, and ohmigod, I did it again! The baby!"

A twinge of unease settled between his shoulders. Darcy sounded happy, but was something wrong with the baby? Using his sternest voice to make her focus, he said, "Tell me."

"The baby kicked! It was so exciting. Abby got up to give me a hug, you know, because I was leaving, and when she stood up from her chair, she grabbed her belly. I thought something was wrong, but she said no, she didn't know what it was. Then she said she thought the baby might be kicking. She didn't know because she hadn't felt it before, just some weird rumbly kind of feelings, but she put her hand on her side, and it kicked!"

Glen closed his eyes against gathering moisture.

"And she let me feel it. Dad, it was so exciting! Have you felt a baby kick before? Of course, you have. Anyway, I never have, and it was grrreaaat! I can't believe I'm going to have a little brother or sister this fall. This is the best thing that's ever happened to me."

He didn't have any words for that.

The next words from Darcy were subdued. "Dad? You're going to get back together with her, aren't you?"

"I am," he said with absolute conviction.

****

Glen arrived fifteen minutes after the baby shower at The Gables began. He knew what time it was because Jason had told him. Linda had told him. Darcy had told him. Hell, some of them might even be there, which made what he had planned even more terrifying.

He leaned against the roof of his car and took a big gulp of humidity. The summer sun beat down on his head, perspiration rolled down his back, and bees humming in the flowerbeds added to the ringing in his ears. When he pushed away from the vehicle and made his way to The Gables front entrance, his legs shook.

He didn't knock on the front door. It was an inn, after all, so even if he observed that formality, it was unlikely anyone would hear him.

Inside the lobby reminded him of another day. When snow covered the hillside and Abby glowed with life. Jason had promised to keep an eye on her while he got his act together. He said she was okay, but if she was even half as lost as he was without her—

"What are you doing here?" Romney glared at him over the batwing doors.

This could be a battle he didn't need when the biggest one still lay ahead of him, so Glen chose his words with care. "I'm here to apologize."

"And?"

"And make Abby happy for the rest of her life if she'll still have me."

David emerged from the dining room to his right. "Good answer." He turned to a younger man standing behind him. With reddish-brown hair and thick blue glasses, he could only be Hume. "What do you think?" David asked him.

"I don't know. What do you think?" Hume looked to Romney, who was no longer glaring but instead scowled at Glen.

"I think we'd better go with him. In case Abby needs backup."

With fraternal entourage in tow, or guards depending on how you looked at them, Glen walked down the hall toward the back dining room.

He could hear the party in progress. It sounded like a big crowd. When he entered through the archway, everyone would see him. All eyes would be on him as effectively as if he were on stage.

His hands grew clammy. The room dipped and swayed, the artwork on the walls going in and out of focus.

"You all right?" Hume asked with concern.

Glen grabbed the corner of the piano and took a deep breath. If he tried to speak, he might throw up all over the thick oriental runner.

"Glen?"

Hearing David's voice helped him recover some control. He let go of the piano and shook his hands, deliberately trying to relax his muscles so he could cross the eight or ten feet remaining between where he stood and that archway.

"I'm okay," he croaked. Then, to the three men still staring at him, he explained, "Glossophobia."

"Say what?" This from Romney.

"Fear of public speaking," Hume explained.

So, he was smart like his big sister.

Thoughts of Abby centered him even more and gave him the strength to cross the portal into the back dining room. The bridal shower guests stopped talking. He didn't know if there were five people in the room or twenty. The only one that mattered to him sat before the fireplace surrounded by cast-off wrapping paper. Her gray-green eyes were wide with shock. Her chestnut hair was piled up on her head in a sloppy bun, and she wore a shapeless, green top that made her look four feet wide. He wanted to scoop her up and run away with her.

Someone nudged him in the shoulder none too gently. Romney, reminding him that he should speak.

"Sorry to crash your party, Sara."

"Don't you dare apologize to *me*." The implication being that he owed one to someone else.

He cleared his throat and focused on Abby. "Sixteen years ago, I stood in that courthouse in Guildhall and thought my life was over. My marriage was ending. I wasn't going to see my kids every day, wasn't even going to see my daughter born, and the circumstances of my divorce meant that I would have to leave the Northeast Kingdom and start a career away from everyone who meant anything to me."

From the corner of his eye, he saw Linda exchange a glance with his mother. Even his *mother* was here.

Momentarily distracted, he scanned the guests for the first time. Some he recognized. Trevor's girlfriend Amy sat next to Sara holding a notebook and pen, presumably the gift log.

No one seemed surprised to see him.

"You were saying?" Linda nudged him verbally.

"Right." Meeting Abby's gaze, he continued. "It was the worst day imaginable, but one good thing came out of it. There was this girl clerking for the judge. She had gray-green eyes, thick chestnut hair, and a body—"

He looked at his mother, remembered Abby's brothers behind him, and felt color staining his cheeks. "Never mind about that. What's important is I never forgot her. Let's just say she set a precedent for me that day. No one else could compare to her or measure up to that memory. And it seems she never forgot me, either."

Abby no longer looked shocked, but she did look wary, and who could blame her? A declaration of infatuation was less than she deserved. She probably thought it was all he had to offer.

Advancing into the room, he came to a stop in front of her, wrapping paper at his feet and a frilly decoration suspended from the ceiling bounced against the side of his head.

"I love you, Abby."

She bit her lower lip, eyes swimming with tears. He didn't want to ever make her cry again, so he continued before she could say love wasn't enough.

"I bought the cottage behind Jason and Sara's house. I've already got contractors lined up to start renovations and additions to make it big enough for a family. Colin and Darcy are enrolled in Somerset Academy for the fall term, but now they won't have to live with my parents when it starts."

He couldn't define the look that crossed her face. Was she thinking he would take care of his kids but not their child? Did she understand the significance of him telling her this in front of an audience?

"They can live in the cottage. I took the position Trevor was training for in Sherbrooke so I can commute to and from work every day. It's only about an hour drive even with the border crossing. I'll be living in the cottage with the kids, home every night."

Kicking aside some of the wrapping paper, he took a deep breath and dropped down onto the cleared space. "I told you once that I would get down on my knees and beg if I had to. And since I've been about as stupid as a man can be, you deserve to see me begging."

She lifted one hand toward him then dropped it into her lap. Hope and fear shone through her tears.

"Abby, our home won't be complete without you in it." Taking her small hand, he kissed the tips of her fingers. "Will you marry me, and move into the cottage with us? Raise our baby together?"

"Babies," she whispered. So softly he wasn't sure he heard her right.

"What?"

A watery chuckle spilled from her luscious lips. "Babies," she said more clearly. "We're having twins."

****

Abby sat beside Glen on the floor, his head propped on her thigh like a pillow. She stroked his dark curls until his blue eyes fluttered open.

"Did you say yes?"

She brushed his stubbled cheek, unable to stop touching him, but they still had a lot to clear up before she gave him her answer. "I have some questions for you first."

"Of course. Anything."

"Are you sorry for being an ass?" Her eyes teared up again. Hormones.

"I'm sorry."

"You hurt me more than anyone has ever hurt me in my life."

He reached up and grasped her hand. "I'm so sorry."

"I should think so." Clearing the tears from her throat, she pressed, "And you'll never do it again?"

"Never."

"Good, because I might let Romney castrate you if you do."

"I'm here for you, little sister." Her brother grinned from the doorway.

Glen's gaze never strayed from her face. "Pathos got the better of logos in this case," he admitted, reminding her of their conversation.

"Oh, geez, he speaks her language," Romney muttered. "Translation, please?"

Abby's heart soared. Smiling for what felt like the first time in months, she explained, "He would only succumb to emotion if his heart was involved and at risk. He wasn't thinking with his brain."

"So, it's a good thing that he made an idiot of himself? First rejecting you and now falling at your feet. I mean, literally falling at your feet?"

"It tells me all I need to know about his feelings."

Glen sat up and laced his fingers through hers. "I've answered your questions, judge. You've heard my case. Are you ready to share your verdict?"

"You heard the part about twins, right?"

"I didn't just faint from public speaking." Everyone laughed. "Mostly, but the twin thing didn't help."

"And you'll raise them the way you have Colin and Darcy? Love them and guide them until they are all grown up?"

"I will."

"Me too," Darcy added. "I want to help. I'm the youngest cousin, and it really stinks sometimes. I can't wait to be a big sister. Please say yes, Abby?"

"Thank you, sweetheart." Abby smiled at the teenager, then returned her attention to him.

"I've already picked out names." It was a challenge with a purpose.

"Okay."

"Her full name is Mutia Grace, after my grandmothers. We can call her Grace."

He squeezed her hand. "I like it."

"And Justin, because I love the law."

He nodded.

"His full name will be Justin Douglas Plankey."

Now he swallowed and his blue eyes misted over. He had told her once that every first son in the Plankey family was given the middle name Douglas, but his ex-deprived him of that privilege when Colin was born.

"You love me," he correctly surmised.

Stretching over her belly to reach him, she kissed his lips and said, "I love you, Glen Plankey."

He returned her kiss, then leaned away and frowned. "There's still one more question to be answered."

Stroking the side of his cheek, she gave him what he was waiting for. "The answer is yes. I said yes."

The End

Thank you for reading Precedent for Passion, Book One in my Love in the Kingdom series. If you enjoyed this story, please consider leaving a review for other readers where you purchased this book.
You can continue the series with:
Tender Possession-Book Two
(Romney and Emmeline-excerpt on the next page)
Open Door to Love-Book Three
(David and Jonnie)
A Full-Bodied Love-Book Four
(Roger and Lisa)
Learn more about my work at:
https://www.amber-cross.com[1]

---

1. https://www.amber-cross.com/

PRECEDENT FOR PASSION

Excerpt from Tender Possession

"You'll be coming to Andros, then?"

Unsnapping her coat, she brushed by him and hung it up, buying time. "I think we need to get some things straight first. Some boundaries."

"Oh?"

She stepped back a few feet to look directly at him. "I don't want to sleep with you."

"Yes, you do."

His arrogance momentarily left her at a loss for words. Recovering quickly, she said, "I mean I'm not going to sleep with you."

"Is there something wrong with me?" He cocked his head to the side and ran his gaze down the length of his body, then up again.

"Something I should know about?"

Nonplussed, she said, "No, there's nothing wrong with you."

His smile was blinding. Deep grooves formed on either side of his mouth, and his dark eyes lit with humor. She had to admit she fell right into that one even before he said, "Then you do want to sleep with me."